Baiting HIM

Shooting Stars Series

Fighting to Breathe
Wide Open Spaces
One Last Wish

Fluke My Life Series

Running into Love
Stumbling into Love
Tossed into Love
Drawn into Love

How to Catch an Alpha Series

Catching Him
Baiting Him
Hooking Him (coming soon)

Writing as C. A. Rose

Alfha Law Series

Justified
Liability
Verdict

Stand-Alone Title

Finders Keepers

Baiting HIM

Aurora Rose Reynolds

 Montlake

Published by Montlake, Seattle
www.apub.com

Amazon, the Amazon logo, and Montlake are trademarks of Amazon.com, Inc., or its affiliates.

ISBN-13: 9781542010214
ISBN-10: 1542010217

Cover design by Letitia Hasser

Cover photography by Wander Aguiar Photography

Printed in the United States of America

To anyone searching for happiness

Suggestion 1

LEAVE HIM WANTING MORE

CHRISSIE

"I'm so happy for you, Leah," I tell my best friend while accepting two shot glasses from the waitress.

"I still can't believe I'm actually getting married, Chrissie." She shakes her head, making her dark hair appear to shimmer in the flashing lights, and her blue eyes brighten with happiness as she holds out her hand to look at the large diamond on her ring finger.

She might not be able to believe that she's getting married, but I can. I knew the moment I saw Tyler and her together for the first time that there was something special between them. I couldn't be happier for her, especially after witnessing firsthand some of her previous disastrous relationships.

"Here's to your happily ever after." I raise my shot glass toward her.

She holds up hers in return and smiles. "And here's to you finding yours."

I smile, too, even though I doubt love is in the cards for me. I could blame my lack of enthusiasm for finding love on men in general being jerks—which, more often than not, they are—but I'm mostly to blame. I work all the time and rarely have time to myself; plus, I don't put a lot of effort into meeting men. Whenever I have a free moment, I use that time wisely to sleep instead of scanning dating sites and going out. Thinking about it now, I don't remember the last time I went out on a real date. Unless you consider meeting up with someone for a quick coffee in the middle of the day a date.

"Are you two going to sit in this corner all night and chat, or are you actually going to join the bachelorette party?" our friend Ivy asks, glancing between Leah and me.

"Sorry, we were having a moment." Leah laughs, and I giggle.

Ivy rolls her eyes at the two of us, then holds out her hand. "Have your moment later. Let's go dance." As soon as Leah places her hand in Ivy's, she drags her up off the couch and pulls her out onto the dance floor.

Even in the large crowd of dancing people, I have no problem spotting all the girls we came here with tonight. Just like me, they're wearing flashing penis necklaces and penis earrings. We look ridiculous, but as Leah's maid of honor, I wanted to give her the full bride-to-be experience, including lots of penises and a sash with bold lettering that says **SAME PENIS FOREVER**. Maybe the sash was overkill, but whatever; it made her soon-to-be-husband grin and her crack up when I put it on her.

While everyone's on the dance floor, I get up from the couch and look for the sign for the restroom, which is located in the rear of the club. I wobble in that direction, a little unsteady on my feet from the alcohol I've consumed. Thank goodness Tyler agreed to be our designated driver and pick us up whenever we're ready to leave.

After standing in line for at least twenty minutes, I sigh. Every woman in the place seems to be waiting to go to the restroom, and the longer I stand there, the more urgent my need becomes. I spot the men's restroom a little farther down the hall, and of course there's no line. I watch the door closely and notice that every guy who goes in seems to come out within a few minutes.

Screw it, I tell myself and head down the hall. When the last guy I saw go in exits, I step inside and rush across the empty room to one of the stalls. I pee quickly while listening for the sound of the door opening and make sure the coast is clear before leaving the stall to wash my hands.

Just as I'm reaching for a paper towel, the door opens. I turn to apologize for invading the men's room, but the words get stuck on my tongue because the most attractive man I've ever seen enters. I blink, wondering if he's a figment of my imagination or if I'm dreaming, because there is no way he's real. He's so tall his head is just a few inches from the top of the doorway, and his shoulders are so broad they seem to fill the space.

He frowns at me, causing his dark brows to knit together over his green eyes. Then he looks around as if to make sure he's not in the women's room, giving me a side view of his sharply angled jaw.

"You're not in the wrong place. I am," I assure him, and his gaze returns to me. "The line for the ladies' room was long, so I snuck in here when it was empty."

"Are you finished, or do you need me to guard the door?" he asks, seeming genuine, which is surprising, coming from a guy who looks like he does.

Touched by the offer, I reply, "That's sweet, but I'm all done." I smile as I toss the paper towel into the overflowing trash can. He opens the door, holding his hand up high enough that I won't need to duck under his arm to get out. Once I'm in the hall, I look over my shoulder at him and smile once more. "Thanks."

"No problem, sweetheart." He winks, and my stomach flutters.

Like any smart woman dealing with a man who is far too attractive, I ignore the flutter and head back down the hall. The girl who was ahead of me is still in line for the women's restroom, and when she realizes where I've just come from, she frowns.

I stop near her, then whisper, "I used the men's room. There wasn't a line. Also, just a guess, but it's probably a lot cleaner than the women's room."

"Thanks," she whispers back, then looks around before she gets out of line. I wonder if I should warn her about the man in there now, but then I shrug. She'll figure it out on her own. I walk around the edge of the dance floor, searching the crowd for my friends until I spot them all dancing together, and then I join them.

An hour later, with my feet killing me and my throat dry, I shout over the music into Leah's ear while I motion toward the bar. "I'm going to get a drink. Do you want anything?"

"No!" she shouts back, grinning drunkenly.

"All right, I'll be back."

She nods, and I move off the dance floor and fumble my way through the crowd, saying "Excuse me" and "Sorry" dozens of times. When I finally reach the bar, I let out a happy sigh when I see an open stool. I take a seat and wait for one of the three bartenders to notice me. This—I know from experience—will take a while, because unlike most of the extraordinarily beautiful men and women here, I'm not special in any way.

I'm five three on a good day and have brown hair that is confused about whether it's wavy or straight and sits just past my shoulders. My eyes, which are one of my more unique qualities, are hazel in color. My face is cute in a chubby cherub kind of way, and I'm plump. I'm not exactly overweight, but I do carry extra pounds that are the result of owning a bakery and enjoying the treats I make a little too much.

"Do you think maybe next time you'll not tell every fucking woman in my club that they should use the men's room?"

The question is growled into my ear, and I spin around on my stool to face the man pressed against my back, which brings us face to face.

"What?" I blink, trying to focus on him, but with the lights flashing every few seconds and the alcohol that's still in my system, it's not exactly easy to do.

"The line for the men's room is now just as long as the one for the ladies', since you made your exit and shared your wisdom about it being empty and clean."

"Oh." I bite my lip, and his eyes drop to my mouth.

"Yeah, oh." They slide back up to meet mine.

"I'm sorry, but in my defense, I only told one person." I hold up a finger, and his eyes narrow on it between us.

"Yeah, and as usual with women, that shit went viral in about two point five seconds."

"Did you say this is your club?" I ask, leaning back, not sure I heard him correctly. He looks young. Not as young as me, but definitely young.

"Yeah."

"Then maybe you should think about having a couple more restrooms put in."

"Thanks for the advice, sweetheart. I'll be sure to get on that."

Even though I know he's being sarcastic, I still smile and chirp, "You're welcome."

His gaze lowers, skimming over my tight black dress. Without thinking, I cross my legs, causing my dress to ride up my thighs, and his jaw seems to twitch in response. Even though I tell myself I feel nothing, I still feel the flutter between my legs, and my heartbeat seems to pick up speed.

"Fuck," he rumbles right before his gaze meets mine once more.

"If that's all, I'm kind of busy trying to get one of the bartenders to notice me," I tell him, and his eyes narrow; then he lifts his head and lets out a loud whistle.

"What can I get for you, boss?" a man asks behind me, and I turn to look over my shoulder at one of the three bartenders behind the bar.

"Water," the guy in my personal space orders, and I frown.

"Got it." The bartender nods, reaches below the bar, and sets a bottle of water on the wooden surface before moving away.

"I actually wanted a glass of wine," I state, turning to face the man who's too hot, too close, and smells too good for my sanity.

"What's your name?" he asks, reaching around my side and then handing me the bottle after he's unscrewed the lid.

"Pardon?" I take it from him.

"Your name—what is it?"

"Chrissie," I say, taking a sip and enjoying the way the cold water feels on my throat as I swallow.

"Chrissie." My name rolls off his tongue slowly. "Nice to meet you, Chrissie. I'm Gaston, but most people call me Gus."

I blink. "Did you just say your name is Gaston?"

"Yeah."

"Oh my God," I whisper, horrified. "You're like the worst villain ever."

"What?" He looks equal parts offended and confused.

"No one looks like Gaston. No one cooks like Gaston. No one refuses to read a good book like Gaston," I sing.

He chuckles. "Pretty sure those aren't the words to that song, babe."

"You get the point," I mumble.

"Yeah." He suddenly seems closer than before. "I'm guessing by your getup that one of your girlfriends is getting married and you're here celebrating with her."

"Why do you say that?" I pretend to look confused, like I don't know what he's talking about.

"I don't know . . . maybe the penises gave it away?" He smiles.

Lord, he has a great smile. Full lips that showcase his straight white teeth. And with him this close, I can smell his earthy yet dark and mysterious scent. God, I need to get away from him, and soon.

"Obviously, you are not up to date on what's trending," I say, wondering if my voice really sounds as breathy as I think it does. "Penises are all the rage this season."

"Aren't penises always the rage?" he asks with a straight face.

I start to laugh, then stop when I notice he's studying me with an odd expression on his face. "What?"

"What?" he repeats, never taking his eyes from mine.

"Why are you looking at me like that?"

"Because I really fucking want to kiss you, but I'm thinking that would not go over very well, especially with every one of my employees watching us right now."

I ignore his comment about wanting to kiss me, because I can't deal with that, and focus on what he said about people watching us. I look around, feeling heat creep up my cheeks. There are at least a dozen or more people watching us. "Um . . . I think maybe you should go away," I suggest.

"Did you just say I should go away?" he asks, sounding surprised.

I meet his gaze once more and nod. "Yeah, I mean, you're the boss. You're not exactly setting a good precedent with your employees by standing around and chatting."

"I can't tell if you're being serious or not." His lips twitch.

"I'm being serious." I nod. "I mean, I talk to my customers at the bakery all the time, but that's a little different. I mean, no one comes to my bakery, gets smashed, and ends up having a one-night stand. Or as far as I know, that hasn't happened. Not that you can get smashed eating baked goods," I mumble.

"You own a bakery?"

"Yeah, the Sweet Spot, on Main Street."

"The Sweet Spot?" He gets the same look in his eyes that every man gets when they hear the name of my shop.

"I sell cakes and cookies and stuff, not sex toys. So you can get that look off your face." I roll my eyes.

He grins, and I have to admit it's way better than his regular smile. Still, I need to end this. I know guys like him: guys who look great and are pros at having a conversation. They know how to make a woman feel validated and important . . . up until the morning after, when you wake up next to them. After that, all their good qualities fly out the window, and you're left wondering what happened to the guy you met the night before.

Been there, done that, and I'm so not going back for seconds or thirds.

"I need to go find my friends." I hop off the barstool, then look up at him once more. "Thanks for the water, and it was really nice meeting you."

Before he can reply, I leave him without a second glance.

I bob my head to the music playing in the background while rolling balls of snickerdoodle dough through cinnamon sugar, dropping each one on a cookie sheet. When I hear the chime for the front door, I stop what I'm doing to listen. Rachelle and Aubrey are both out front, but they might be too busy to greet the customer who just came in, since for some reason Wednesdays are one of the busiest days at the shop.

When I hear "Holy cow!" screeched loudly in unison, I quickly wash my hands and head out to see what's going on. Standing at the counter, holding the largest, most beautiful bouquet I have ever seen, is Mikey, the older gentleman who runs orders for the florist down the block.

"Hey, Mikey."

"Hey, girl." He smiles. "I think you've got an admirer."

"What?"

"These are for you, hon," he says, and I feel both girls turn to look at me.

"What?" I repeat. I expected him to say the bouquet was for one of my employees. Both Rachelle and Aubrey are in high school. They are beautiful and on the cheerleading team . . . or squad—whatever you want to call it. And judging by the number of cute boys who come in here while they're working, they're both popular.

"These are for you," he repeats as he sets the flowers on the counter. "Can you sign this?"

I scribble my name, then examine the flowers for a card as Mikey says "Later" and heads out.

"Who are they from?" Rachelle asks.

"It's not your birthday," Aubrey says, telling me something I know.

"I don't know who they're from, and no, it's not my birthday." I finally spot a small envelope between a bunch of peonies. I open it and slide the card out, reading the words three times, since I'm positive I'm seeing things.

I haven't been able to stop thinking about you. I hope you're having the same problem.

Call me,

Gaston

His number is neatly printed at the bottom.

"So who are they from?" Rachelle asks, jumping up and down excitedly at my side.

"Um . . ." I glance at her, then at the flowers. He remembered not only my name but also the name of my shop, and then he sent me flowers—something I don't think any man has ever done for me before. An odd sense of excitement begins to fill my chest.

"Obviously, whoever they're from has serious fricking class, because this bouquet must have cost, like, over two hundred dollars," Aubrey observes.

I swallow and look back down at the card once again.

"So tell us who they're from," Rachelle repeats.

"A guy I met on Saturday." I lean forward to smell a yellow rose. "I . . . we . . . I don't know. We spoke, and he was very nice and funny. I just didn't think I would ever hear from him again."

"Wasn't Saturday Leah's bachelorette party?" Aubrey asks.

"It was; that's where I met him. He owns the club we went to," I answer, blown away by the flowers. Seriously, they are beautiful.

"So you just spoke to him one time, and he sent you flowers?" Aubrey looks a little confused. Heck, I'm confused too. I've never had a guy send me flowers after a date, so I would never expect them after a short conversation.

"Of course he sent her flowers." Rachelle rolls her eyes. "He wanted to make a statement, because she's hot and he knows tons of guys want her."

"Hashtag retweet." Aubrey nods and then asks, "Did he send his number?"

I look between both girls, wondering what universe they live in. Tons of guys don't want me. Heck, not even one guy wants me. "Um . . ."

"Did he?" Rachelle prompts.

"Are you going to call him?" Aubrey continues.

"He sent it, but I don't know." Yes, he was easy to talk to, funny, and charming, but I'm not sure if he is *actually* interested in me or if he's interested because I didn't immediately fall at his feet, which I'm sure happens often. Being as good looking as he is and owning a club is a double whammy. I have no doubt that beautiful women are always coming on to him and telling him exactly what he wants to hear.

"Was he hot?" Rachelle asks.

"Very." I nod.

"So are you playing hard to get?" she asks.

"No, honey, I'm not playing any games. I'm just trying to look out for myself. Sometimes men will show you what they think you want to see, and then once they get you in their grasp, you figure out it was all a lie."

"But what if it's not a lie?" Aubrey prompts. "I mean, I don't know very many guys who would send flowers to a woman after only just talking to her. My dad doesn't even send flowers to my mom, and they've been married like forever and ever."

"I think you should call him," Rachelle says.

"I'll think about it." I look around. The four high tables near the front window are now empty following our after-school rush, and the only customers in the shop are a mom and her son, sitting at one of the kid tables. Judging by the amount of icing on the little boy's face, he's enjoying his cupcake, and his mom is talking on the phone. "Do you girls mind finishing up the cookies in the back? I need to put the finishing touches on Leah's cake so I can pack it up tonight and drive it down to Tennessee tomorrow for the wedding."

"For sure," Aubrey agrees with a smile that matches Rachelle's. Both girls love baking, but normally I'm done with everything by the time they come in after school, so they don't always get to help out with that.

"Don't forget—my mom will be here tomorrow. She knows you're both coming in at noon and are pretty much in charge. She's promised not to step on your toes."

"We love your mom. And don't worry—everything will be okay. You should just focus on having a good time," Rachelle says.

"I know it will be," I agree. Then I add, "Now go make cookies."

I laugh at the girls as they jump and dance their way to the back kitchen. I wasn't sure about hiring two high school girls to work for me, but it was one of the best decisions I've made, and not just because their friends are always coming in to hang out—which means they spend money while they're here. No, both girls are hardworking, sweet, and dependable. I work so much that I see them more than I see my family or even my best friend, so we're close . . . or as close as a thirty-three-year-old woman can be with two seventeen-year-old girls.

One thing I know for sure is it's going to suck when I lose them after this summer, when they both go away for college. With a heavy sigh, I grab a few napkins and dampen them, then walk across the shop and hand them to the mom, who mouths *Thank you* before cleaning off her son's cute little face. I head back to the counter, straightening up along the way.

Ever since I was five, I knew I wanted to own a bakery, and my parents took me seriously enough to start saving money for me. When I graduated from high school, they told me what they'd done but said they wouldn't give me access to the funds until after I'd completed culinary school and a few business-management classes. I agreed and went to one of the best culinary schools in New York City and took night classes for business management. After I graduated, I moved back home and got a job at a café in town to gain experience; then I worked my way up to manager. I was there for almost ten years, and during that time I saved enough to open the Sweet Spot.

I have never regretted my decision, not for a single day. Even now, as I look around at the bright-yellow chairs and cupcake-shaped napkin dispensers sitting in the middle of pink tables as well as the cupcakes brightly painted on the walls of my shop, I know I'm living a dream come true.

Now I just need to finish up my best friend's wedding cake and get it to Tennessee so I can watch her marry that man of hers. I'll figure out what to do about Gaston when I get home.

Suggestion 2

Go After What You Want

GASTON

"What?" I bark at the knock on my office door.

"Jesus, what crawled up your ass?" my best friend, Luke, asks while closing the door before walking across the room to take a seat opposite me.

"Nothing. What did you need?" I lean back in my chair and rub the bridge of my nose in an attempt to get rid of the headache that's been steadily building behind my eyes for the past few days.

"Is your piss-poor attitude because of the chick you sent flowers to?" He studies me, and my jaw clenches and unclenches. "I'm gonna go out on a limb and guess by your sunny demeanor that she still hasn't called."

No, she hasn't called, and that shouldn't piss me off, but it does. I don't even know the woman who's suddenly consumed my mind. But what I do know is she's gorgeous, with a beautiful full figure my hands and mouth itch to explore and a sense of humor that makes my dick hard. "Did you need something, or are you just here to annoy me?"

"Just go to her job and talk to her," he says, ignoring my question.

"Yeah, that wouldn't be awkward." I scrub my hand through my hair. "I sent her flowers with my number and haven't heard from her." I shake my head and do the math. It's been five days since I sent the bouquet. "She's obviously not interested." Isn't that a kick to the gut? The first woman I'm actually interested in pursuing isn't interested in me.

"Cammy didn't want anything to do with me when we met; she thought I was a player and was just trying to get into her pants."

"You were a player, and you were trying to get into her pants," I point out.

"I was a player until I met her. Getting in her pants was a bonus." He shrugs while grinning; then he sits forward with a serious look on his face. "The point is, I didn't let her push me away and I didn't give up, because I knew she was as into me as I was her. I just had to convince her to see things my way."

"You mean you stalked her until she agreed to go out with you."

"You say it like it's a bad thing."

"Stalking is illegal."

"It worked, didn't it?" he asks with a knowing smirk.

Shit, he's right.

"Go by her shop tomorrow and ask her out. If she says no, go back again the next day and the next until she agrees."

"You might be a little insane," I inform him.

"Maybe. Then again, I have the wife I wanted and a beautiful little girl at home who calls me Daddy, so things worked out for me in the end."

"True," I mumble, wondering if I should take his advice. The truth is, I know Chrissie had to have felt what I felt when we met. At least I really fucking hope she did. I swallow as doubt settles deep in my chest.

"I've never seen you like this, so you must really like this chick," he says quietly.

"I do." In the few minutes I spent with her, she made me laugh, frustrated me, and had me so on edge with desire that I was tempted to throw her over my shoulder and take her someplace quiet where I could kiss her without interruption.

"I—"

Before he can say more, there's another knock on the door.

"Hold that thought," I say, looking at him before I shout, "Come in!"

"Hey, Gus." Georgia, my bar manager, walks in with a bright smile that quickly slides away when she spots Luke sitting across from me. "Luke."

"Georgia." He lifts his chin, then leans back in the chair, crossing his arms over his chest. I'm not surprised by either of their reactions, since they don't like each other and only tolerate being in each other's company because they both work for me.

"Did you need something?" I ask when she stops in the middle of the room.

"I just wanted to go over the schedule for next week with you."

"I got it when you emailed it to me. I emailed you back, letting you know it looked good."

"Oh, I didn't see that you replied," she says, and Luke makes a noise of disbelief that causes her to turn to look at him with what I'm guessing is a murderous expression.

"Did you need anything else?" I ask, and her features soften as her eyes come back to me.

"Um, no, not that I can think of."

"If that's all, I'll be out in a bit after I finish up some paperwork."

"Sure. Let me know if you need anything."

"Will do," I agree, and she nods once before quickly turning around and leaving my office.

"Dude, you seriously need to deal with that situation." Luke shakes his head.

"There's no situation to deal with—she's my employee."

"Yeah, but in her mind, you're eventually going to see that she's the kind of woman you can take home to your mama, put a ring on and a baby in."

"That's never gonna happen," I say, my stomach actually turning at the thought.

"I know that and you know that, but she sure as fuck believes something different."

"I'll deal with it," I sigh, knowing he's right but also hoping she will realize nothing is ever going to happen between us.

"Jesus, I'm so fucking happy I'm married," he rumbles, making me chuckle.

"Luke 'Forever Single' Parker, happy he's married." I laugh.

"You'll find the right woman one day, and then you'll understand exactly why I'm happy to be off the market." He stands up and places his hands on my desk before leaning over it. "Get your girl, because if you don't and I have to deal with your shitty attitude for another day, I'm kidnapping her and tying her to your bed."

"Does Cammy know exactly how insane you are?"

"Yep, and she loves it. She'd probably help me kidnap your girl if I asked her to then fuck me senseless when it was done."

Knowing Cammy as I do, I'm sure she would help him and get off on it. "Get out of my office—I have shit to do."

"Was leaving anyway." He grins before he shuts the door behind himself.

I glance at the clock on the wall and calculate exactly how many hours it will be until I see Chrissie again. The double-digit number makes me groan. With no other choice, I get back to work, hoping like fuck that I can convince the woman who has completely taken over my every waking thought to take a chance on me.

Suggestion 3

GIVE A LITTLE

CHRISSIE

"The wedding looked beautiful, and you were killer in your dress," Rachelle tells me while scrolling through the photos I took at Leah's wedding. "Also"—she waves the last bit of cookie in her hand between us—"whatever this is, it's delicious."

I can't help but smile as she shoves the last bite of my newest creation into her mouth. "It's a mixture of banana chips and dark chocolate cookie dough."

"Well, it should totally go in the showcase."

"Maybe next week. I think I want to play with it a little more—maybe add peanut butter chips to the mix and see how it tastes."

"Oh, I want to try that," she says and then hands me back my phone.

I slide through some of the photos, stopping on one I took of Leah before she walked down the aisle. Even in the photo, I can feel her happiness and excitement.

"Oh my God," Rachelle hisses suddenly, jabbing her elbow into my rib cage and catching me off guard.

"What the heck?" I wheeze, grabbing hold of my side, sure I'm going to have a bruise there.

"Oh my God, oh my God, he's coming in!" she cries, and I look to see which one of the dozens of high school boys she likes is about to enter the shop.

My eyes widen and my stomach drops when it's not some high school kid, but Gaston . . . sweaty, gorgeous Gaston in running shoes, sweats cut off at the knee, and a hoodie.

"Please tell me he's not too old for me," she breathes.

"Why don't you check to see if Aubrey needs any help in the back? And I'm sure the muffins are ready to come out of the oven by now."

"My parents say I'm mature for seventeen. Maybe that means they'd be cool with me dating an older guy," she whispers just loud enough for me to hear.

I fight back laughter and order, "Rachelle, go check the muffins before I call your dad."

"Oh, all right." She gives in but not before she checks him out one more time. I roll my eyes at her, and she shrugs as I feel Gaston's presence getting closer to the counter.

When she's out of sight, I turn my head and all rational thoughts leave my mind. Anything I might have said gets stuck on the tip of my tongue as an electric current crackles between us, causing the hair on my arms and the back of my neck to stand on end. Once again faced with the full force of his beauty up close—only now in the bright light of day—I'm at a loss. I didn't forget how attractive he is; I just assumed that my drunken mind had made him out to be hotter than he really is.

"Hey," I finally get out as his gaze bores into mine.

"You got a minute to talk?"

I look around to make sure that the shop is empty, then tip my head to the side. "Is it okay if we talk here?"

"Yeah, this is fine." He lifts his hand and runs his fingers through his damp hair. "You haven't called."

I fight back the urge to flinch from his tone and then clear my throat. "Sorry, I should have called to tell you thank you for the flowers. They were beautiful. Actually, they still are beautiful."

"I'm not talking about you calling to thank me for the flowers. I'm talking about you not calling me at all. Are you seeing someone?"

My head jerks back from the underlying tone of frustration in his question, and I shake my head while answering. "No."

"Are you attracted to me?"

"What?" Who asks someone something like that?

"I'm trying to figure out why I haven't heard from you." His eyes are filled with annoyance and bore into mine. "I thought we hit it off. No one has made me laugh the way you did. I know that even if you say you're not attracted to me, you are. I also know I'm definitely fucking attracted to you."

Is it hot in here? It suddenly feels really hot in here. I want to touch my cheeks to feel if they're red, and I just barely contain the urge.

"So why haven't you called me?"

"Honestly?"

"Well, I can't say I'm real big on the idea of you lying to me," he says dryly, but I still catch a hint of amusement in his eyes.

A smile I can't hold in tips up the corner of my lips. "I've been trying to figure out if it'd be smart to call you."

"Smart?" His forehead wrinkles with confusion.

"Yeah, smart. I know men and the games they like to play. They all want to catch a woman when she's running, but once they get her in their grasp, the fun is over and they move along, leaving the woman wondering what happened and where things went wrong."

He leans across the counter toward me, and my breath catches as he wraps his finger around a piece of hair that fell out of my ponytail, slowly tucking it behind my ear. "Don't confuse men and boys, sweetheart," he says, then lowers his voice. "And don't assume you know the kind of man I am when you haven't given me a chance to show you what I'm made of."

Goose bumps rise along my skin as a deep, rumbly growl escapes his chest, and his suddenly dark eyes slide to my lips. My pulse skyrockets with desire, and I blurt, "Do you want a cookie?"

He blinks, leaning back out of my space and allowing me to finally breathe normally. "Did you just ask if I want a cookie?"

"Um . . . yes. You seem a little angry. Maybe your blood sugar is low."

His lips twitch into a full smile, and I get a little lightheaded from the sight. "Do you have plans this evening?" he asks.

"Why?"

"Because I want to take you out to dinner or get a coffee with you. Honestly, at this point, I don't care what we do, as long as I get to spend some time with you, one on one, when neither of us is working."

With a sudden giddiness racing through my system, I study him. I don't fully understand why this insanely gorgeous man is pursuing me, but a part of me wants to find out. "I don't have plans, but my shop doesn't close until six. I'd need time to go home and change, so it would be late by the time I could meet you for dinner," I ramble.

I swear I see relief cross his features before he tells me, "You should remember that I own a club. I don't exactly keep normal hours myself. I'm good with a late dinner if you are."

"I'm good with that."

"Where's your cell phone?" I pull it out of the back pocket of my jeans, and he takes it from me, then holds it up to my face to unlock the screen. The next thing I know, he's swiping through it quickly and his cell phone is ringing. "Now I've got your number, and you have mine programmed into your phone. Just send me a message to let me know when you think you'll be ready, and I'll pick you up at your place."

"I can meet you somewhere."

"You've been working all day. I'd rather know you got to and from dinner safe without falling asleep."

"Okay," I agree, not allowing myself to feel the full force of that kind of consideration in case it's just part of a game he might be the champion at playing.

"Now, about that cookie you mentioned earlier. Do you have any oatmeal cinnamon raisin?"

"I do." I grab two from the showcase, put them in a brown paper bag with my logo stamped on the front, and hand it to him.

"How much?" He starts to reach into the pocket of his hoodie.

"Please don't," I say, and he stops. "Those are apology cookies, so they're on the house."

He takes one cookie out of the bag and holds it up to his mouth. "I'd rather have a different form of apology."

"Yeah, and what would that be?"

"A kiss." He bites into the cookie, winking, and my stomach summersaults. "Holy shit."

"What?" I start to reach for the cookie to rip it from his grasp as my mind fills with thoughts of him biting into the shell of an egg or something worse.

He looks at my hand, raises a brow, and states "This is delicious" before taking another bite.

"Did you expect it to suck?" I laugh.

He shrugs one shoulder, takes another bite, and then, once he's chewed and swallowed, he tells me, "My mom made the best cookies I ever tasted . . . up until now." His expression grows playful. "But if you ever tell her I said that, I'll call you a liar."

I laugh again, remembering how easy he is to talk to from the last time we were together and how much he makes me laugh. "So are you a mama's boy?"

"Oh yeah." He doesn't even pretend to deny it.

I cross my arms over my chest and narrow my eyes. "At least tell me I'm not going to find out you live in her basement and depend on her to cook for you and do your laundry."

He chuckles. "No, my mom lives in Jersey in the summer and Florida in the winter. She has more of a social life than I do, and I don't even want to imagine what she'd say or do if I ever asked her to do my laundry. She might cook for me when she's in town, but that's just because she likes to eat and it's a necessity."

"Got it." Just then the shop door opens, and I'm momentarily distracted by the large group of teenagers coming in. They're loud and playful as they claim their usual seats near the front window, placing their bags and coats there before starting for the counter.

"I should let you get to work," Gaston says, gaining my attention once more, and I instantly don't want him to go, which is ridiculous. "Text me, and I'll see you this evening."

"All right, I'll see you this evening," I agree, and he winks before leaving and continuing his jog while holding a paper bag with one less cookie. As soon as he's out of sight, Aubrey and Rachelle rush out of the back kitchen, and both girls jump up and down while holding on to me, which seems to be the only way they know how to react when they are excited.

"Oh my God, he's so totally into you!" Aubrey cries.

"He's funny," Rachelle states and then adds, "and hot."

"So hot," Aubrey agrees, still bouncing on her toes.

"Girls, as much as I love you both, you shouldn't eavesdrop."

"We weren't really eavesdropping. That would mean we were hiding, and we weren't. We were standing in plain sight; you just didn't notice us because of the hot guy." Aubrey smirks.

I laugh, shaking my head, and order, "See what everyone is having. I'm going to go check my emails to make sure I haven't gotten any new inquiries since I've been gone."

"Got it, boss," Rachelle agrees with a goofy salute, and Aubrey goes to grab a pen and paper from the counter.

I leave them to handle things for a while and go to my office. Once I'm seated at my desk, I pull out my cell to call Leah about Gaston but then remember she's still on her honeymoon. I should've told her about Gaston after her bachelorette party, or even when I was with her in Tennessee, but I didn't. If I'd told her about our interaction at the club and the flowers, she would have demanded I call him and give him a chance.

I love my best friend, but since finding love, she's forgotten about the crap even *she* went through when she was on the market and dating. I stare at my phone, wondering who else I can call. Most of my friends have been married for years, and none of them have a clue about dating today. And my mom . . . well, my mom isn't an option. She's still too bitter after my father asked her for a divorce a year ago so he could marry his mistress. Since then, she thinks men should be placed on an island and only used to reproduce. Yes, she actually said that to me. In her defense, she had just finished a bottle of wine and was in her feelings.

With a frustrated sigh, I drop my cell phone on my desk and turn on my computer. I respond to a few emails asking for quotes on birthday and wedding cakes, then go back out to the front of the shop. Even though I trust my girls, I like to remind everyone there is an adult around, even if I rarely have any problems with the kids who come in after school to hang out. It doesn't happen often, but from time to time the boys will get a little out of hand—especially since they, for some reason, think acting loud and rambunctious is a good way to get a girl's attention. I pray they learn with time and wisdom it isn't.

As soon as I step into the front of the shop, I immediately see that every last customer has been taken care of. The group of high schoolers is now seated by the front windows eating, talking, and laughing. There are a few parents with younger children in the corner, an area designed to be closed off from the rest of the shop so parents of toddlers can have a moment to breathe while their littles eat whatever baked good they choose from the display case or color on the walls with chalk. Seeing all is well, I smile at my girls, catching their return grins before they get back to work.

The rest of the day drags, especially after the kids leave, including my employees, who need to make it to a basketball game at which they are cheering. With just a few customers to keep my mind busy, I spend an ungodly amount of time wondering what I should wear tonight.

I'm feeling nervous because Gaston will be here any minute to pick me up for dinner, and my knees wobble as I glance in the mirror. I don't look much different from when he showed up at the bakery this afternoon, which I hope doesn't disappoint him.

I pulled my hair out of my usual ponytail and added a few more waves with the help of my curling wand and hair spray. I coated my lashes with another layer of mascara and applied a pink lip stain to my lips. After working all day, I barely had the energy to shower when I got home, not to mention fixing myself up and changing into the long-sleeved black jumpsuit and heels I'm currently wearing.

The doorbell rings, and I fluff my hair as I walk through my one-bedroom condo. I bought my place because of the view of the ocean from the balcony. It cost me an arm and a leg, and I have to travel down twenty-nine floors to reach the sand. But the price I paid was worth every penny, especially when I get to have my morning coffee or late-night wine while looking out at the ocean.

When I make it to the entryway, I take a second to make sure I'm decent before I check the peephole and open the door.

Once again, I'm caught off guard by just how handsome Gaston is. Even dressed casually in jeans and a button-down gray shirt that does amazing things to his eyes, he still makes my breath catch. When I notice he's carrying two reusable shopping bags in one hand, I blink in confusion, then take a step back when he places his big palm against my stomach, urging me inside.

"I know I said I was taking you out to dinner, but after thinking about it and knowing you've probably been up since early this morning, I decided I should just cook dinner for you here. That way you can go to bed without the hassle of dinner out and the ride back home afterward."

He said a lot, but still I'm stuck on one point. "You're going to cook dinner?" I know I sound confused and concerned, but my dad has never—at least, not that I know of—cooked dinner. Really, the only thing I've seen him use the stove for is to scramble eggs in too much oil and make boxed macaroni and cheese, which should have been okay, considering there were only about three ingredients, but it never was.

"Got the stuff to make seafood risotto. I also picked up chicken, in case you're allergic to seafood."

Who is this man, and seriously, what planet did he come from?

"You okay with that?" he prompts.

"I'm not allergic to seafood," I tell him, and he grins a way-too-hot-for-real-life grin. A grin that does serious things to my girl parts.

"Then show me the way to the kitchen, sweetheart, and keep me company while I cook."

"Sure." I lead him down the hall, wishing I'd known this was going to happen. At least then I would have taken a minute to clean up. My apartment is clean, but there are still random clothes tossed onto the back of the couch, magazines and books open on the coffee table, and half-drunk cups of coffee here and there. And my kitchen is a mess. Crackers, chips, and boxes of cereal have been left open on the counters, and dishes are still in the sink from this morning.

"I'm not normally this messy," I blurt, suddenly feeling on edge as we enter the kitchen, and he stops to look around. "I haven't thought much about anything else but work since I got home from my best friend's wedding in Tennessee yesterday afternoon."

"You have a great view," he tells me, ignoring my statement while dropping the grocery bags onto the counter, then moving to my sliding-glass doors and opening them up. It's freezing, but the night is clear, so the moon and every single star seem to be out, reflecting down on the ocean. "I bet you bought this place for the view."

"I did," I admit, watching as he strolls to the edge of the balcony to rest his hands around the banister. "It's better in the summer, but I still enjoy the view in the winter." I pause. "Though I normally enjoy it through the glass, because it's freezing."

I'm standing just inside with my arms wrapped around myself to fight the cold. Without a word, he comes back in, closing the door. "Growing up in Jersey, I got used to the cold. The winters there are no joke, and it snowed all the time. I barely register the cold here."

"I lived in New York for a while, so I understand."

"The state, or the actual city?" he questions, and I know exactly what he's asking. A lot of people say they live in New York, but not many actually live or have lived in the city itself. True Manhattanites are steadfast in their opinion that there's a difference between living in Manhattan and living in Albany or Buffalo.

"Manhattan."

"What took you to Manhattan?" he asks, stopping close enough that I'm able to notice the slight scruff forming along his jaw and below his cheekbones, making them more pronounced.

"School. I went to the Institute of Culinary Education and was there for a little over a year to complete the baking and arts program."

"So they taught you how to make those cookies?" he asks while he casually takes my hand and pulls me toward the kitchen.

"No, my grandma—my dad's mom—had me helping her in the kitchen as soon as I was able to crack eggs. She taught me everything I know, and when she passed away, she left me an old binder with all my family's recipes—recipes that have been passed down generation after generation. Those cookies you liked so much today were actually made first by my dad's great-great-aunt Flo for her husband. He worked on a farm as a ranch hand and needed a pick-me-up halfway through his day, so she came up with the recipe just for him."

When I finish speaking, I notice we've stopped moving and he's studying me intently.

"Does everything you sell in your shop have a story like that?" he asks, letting me go and moving around the kitchen like he's been in it before. He pulls out one of my flimsy plastic cutting boards from one cupboard, then a pan and a pot from another.

"Most things have a story about who made it and why."

"You should write a cookbook."

"What?" I ask as he sets the pan on the stove, turns it on, and adds a drizzle of olive oil from my fancy jar on the counter.

"You should write a book and use each recipe as part of the story. The story of your family. You could sell it at your shop. I think that would be cool."

My whole body seems to warm with appreciation. I've thought about writing a cookbook, but until this moment, I've never thought about how it would be laid out or exactly what would be in it. His encouragement means more than he could possibly know.

"I actually really love that idea," I admit softly.

He smiles, then jerks his head to the side and orders, "Come here."

"I'm right here."

"Yeah, but I want you close." He dips his head toward the floor. I take one tentative step toward him as he watches, and he shakes his head, then prowls toward me. Once we're close enough to touch, he wraps his hands around my hips and leads me with him, walking me backward across the kitchen. "I want you close," he repeats, and my breath catches as he lifts me off the ground and settles my ass on the counter near the stove.

I watch him, almost in a daze, as he takes items from the shopping bags and begins to prepare dinner. I've never had a man cook for me before, unless you count my dad's horrible attempts in the kitchen.

"Who taught you to cook?" I ask as he dices an onion perfectly before scooping it up in my plastic cutting board and dropping it into the heated olive oil in the pan on the stove.

"My mom. I told you she loves to eat. I didn't mention she's full-blooded Italian. My grandma made sure Mom knew her way around the kitchen. That way, she'd be a good wife to whatever man she made her husband. Only, my mom didn't want a husband. She never married anyone, not even my father, much to my grandmother's disapproval." He winks at me, and my stomach flips. "But she did cook for me. She also taught me everything she knew, because she wanted me to be a good husband to whatever woman I ended up marrying."

I start to giggle, and when the sound turns to laughter, he grins at me. "So you're basically telling me that your mom is awesome."

"Basically," he agrees before he adds a can of diced tomatoes, spices, salt, and risotto to the pan. I study him as he slowly adds in chicken stock, and a delicious smell begins to permeate my senses. Again, I wonder what planet this man came from, because there is no way he can possibly be real.

"So, you own Twilight?" I question, hoping for a little more insight into the man standing a few feet away.

"Yeah, that and a couple bars along the beach," he answers with a shrug, like it's not a big deal. Having looked for locations for the Sweet Spot, I know the real estate along the beach is more than a little expensive. Heck, most of the locations are more than I could afford in this lifetime, even if I saved every penny I made.

I grew up lower-middle class. Both my parents worked when my little brother and I were kids, and they still do to this day. My mom is a secretary at one of the local high schools, and my dad is a hotel manager. They scrimped and put money away for me to be able to open my shop and for my brother to go to college. We both got $20,000, which took years and a lot of them going without to save. Now as an adult and understanding the stress that money brings, I wonder if that's one of the reasons they're no longer together.

"That's impressive," I finally murmur, unsure how to proceed or how to process the fact that he's probably loaded.

His head turns my way, and when his eyes lock with mine, I swear he has once more read my thoughts when he continues. "My mom didn't want to marry my dad, but that doesn't mean he wanted nothing to do with me. He was around as much as he could stomach, considering the fact that he was in love with my mom but she didn't feel the same and made that clear by dating regularly and shoving it down his throat." Oh, man. I suddenly feel sad for his father. "Still, he taught me a lot while I was growing up, during the times I was with him. One of the things I learned from him was how to be smart with money. He showed me how to save, and he helped me get my first loan, and then my second. Since he passed away five years ago, I've used his wisdom and bought into a couple local businesses that were on the edge of foreclosure and worked at making those locations profitable again."

"That's even more impressive," I say, then add, holding his stare when he turns to look at me, "I'm sorry about your dad. I've never lost one of my parents, but I'm sure that isn't something easy to go through."

"It's not, but I have a lot of good memories with him. He was an amazing man and father. I appreciate everything he taught me while he was alive."

"Did he and your mom ever work things out?" I ask, then wish I hadn't. I blurt, "Sorry, stupid question."

"No, they didn't, at least not together. He got married when I was nineteen." He smiles fondly, and my heart does a weird double beat. "Nina gave him the family he was always searching for. She had two girls before she met Dad, and he loved them like his own. I consider both of them my sisters, and I love Nina. She's nothing like my mother, but she was absolutely perfect for my dad in every way. While he was alive, they gave each other happiness and contentment, and together they built a beautiful life." I watch as he pulls in a breath, and I feel my own throat get tight. "That's another lesson I learned from my father."

"What lesson was that?" I question, my voice tight with emotion.

"Nothing is more important than your family. Nothing is more important than the people you love, the people who will be there in good times and bad."

Tears fill my eyes, and I try to fight them back, but I'm not skilled enough to hide them from him. When he notices, he's suddenly not standing in front of the stove but right there in my space, pushing my thighs apart and settling himself between my legs. I cover my face, attempting to hide, but he drags my hands away and forces me to look at him. God, he's so beautiful, and the fact that he's been through what he has only makes me like him and respect him so much more.

"I'm sorry." I swipe the tears off my cheeks, and his expression softens.

"Sorry about crying?"

"Yeah."

"Sweetheart, it's sweet that you're crying over my sob story. Still, I don't like your tears."

"Give me a second, and I'll stop," I tell him, and he starts to laugh. "Why are you laughing?" I cry, with more tears rolling down my cheeks.

"You're adorable." He leans in, touching his lips to mine.

I'm caught off guard by the soft kiss and every emotion rushing through me. My mind spins, and I pray this isn't too good to be real.

Suggestion 4

DON'T LISTEN TO YOUR MAMA

CHRISSIE

I lean back against the arm of my couch and take a sip of wine while Gaston sits a cushion away drinking a beer and chuckling.

"In the end, it worked out," I say, and he shakes his head. "Honestly, it was a life lesson. I'm sure one day my own children will sign me up for some project and forget to mention it until the very last second." I've just told him about the time Aubrey and Rachelle volunteered me to make five hundred cookies for a bake sale to help the high school basketball team travel to an away game in another state. I had no problems with them offering my cookies, but they forgot to mention it to me until the day before the bake sale, which meant I was baking from dusk till dawn without help, since the girls couldn't stay with me all night and had school the next day.

His expression softens at the mention of children, and my fingers tighten around my wineglass. "Let's hope it's not five hundred cookies that you have to bake in one night."

"I hope I never have to do that again, but the silver lining is that my cookies were a hit, and I've had a lot more business since then."

"There's always a silver lining." His eyes brighten, and his lips tip up with humor.

My stomach is stuffed full of the delicious seafood risotto he cooked for us and flips at the sight while my brain replays the way his lips felt when he kissed me earlier. A kiss that ended quickly and since then has felt, at least to me, like an elephant in the room. Not that it's made things uncomfortable or awkward. Our conversation has flowed easily, and we've both laughed a lot tonight.

My mom's designated ringtone begins to play from inside my purse. I sit forward to grab it. "Sorry, it's my mom," I tell him as I search for my phone.

"Do you want me to give you some privacy?"

I focus on him with my cell now in my hand and shake my head. "No, she just likes to check in on me at night sometimes because I live alone."

"Good mom."

"Yeah," I agree, then slide my finger across the screen and place it against my ear. "Hey, Mom."

"He's taking her to Hawaii!" She's so loud that even Gaston can hear her, judging by his surprised expression.

"Who's taking who to Hawaii?" I ask, confused.

"Who do you think?" she yells once again, and an uncomfortable knot starts to tighten within my chest, making it difficult to breathe. "Your father . . . he's . . . he's taking her to Hawaii."

"Mom," I whisper tightly, pulling my eyes from Gaston's questioning gaze. "Calm down."

"How can I calm down? Do you know how many times I asked, begged, and pleaded for him to go away with me? Do you know how many times I told him that I wanted to go to Hawaii *specifically*," she sobs, barely able to continue, "and told him how good it would be for the two of us to get away?"

Pain slashes through me. I love my father, but I can't deny I'm angry with him. Not only for what he did to my mom but to our whole family. I'm old enough to understand that no relationship is ever perfect, but just like my mom, I didn't see my father's betrayal coming. He never let on that he wasn't happy; it was like he one day just decided to turn out the lights and then expected us to be able to navigate through the dark without him.

"Mom, please don't cry," I beg, feeling uncomfortable talking about this with Gaston so close. I get off the couch to put some space between him and me.

"I know I should be okay by now," she whispers, her voice filled with pain. "But every time I think I'm making progress, something else happens and I . . . I remember what I thought we had."

"Mommy," I whisper back, resting my forehead against the sliding door.

"I hate that I still love him." Oh God. Tears fill my eyes, and I attempt to blink them away while looking out at the ocean through my hazy reflection in the glass. "I wish I could hate him. I wish he didn't pretend for years like everything was okay, like *we* were okay, when we weren't. I wish I knew what was happening so I could've prepared for it."

"You can't turn love off and on, but with time things will get easier and the pain will lessen," I say, even though I'm not sure if what I'm saying is true. It's been a year, and my mom is still stuck in the same place emotionally. She's still heartbroken and feeling betrayed.

"Promise me you won't ever trust a man the way I did. Promise me, honey, because I never want to imagine you ever going through something like this."

"Mom—"

"Please, promise me," she pleads, her voice cracking.

"I promise," I say, seeing Gaston's reflection as he gets off the couch and brings my glass and his beer bottle to the kitchen.

"Shit," Mom hisses in my ear.

"What?"

"I didn't realize how late it is. I shouldn't have called you about this tonight." She pauses. "Really, I shouldn't have called you about this at all. I just—"

"It's okay, Mom," I say, cutting her off. "You know I'm here anytime you want to talk."

"It's not okay. I don't want my stupid emotions messing up your relationship with your father. I'll try to do better."

I don't tell her that there isn't a relationship to mess up. Just like he did to my mom, he's pretty much cut me and my brother out of his life. I don't know if it's guilt causing him to keep his distance or if he's trying to erase anything having to do with his old life before he remarried. Whatever it is, it hurts, which is why I try not to think about it at all, and I definitely don't talk to my mom about it. She's emotional enough, and she doesn't need anything else to stress or worry about.

"Get some sleep, honey. I'm sure you're exhausted. We'll talk tomorrow. We can meet for dinner, and you can show me Leah's wedding pictures."

"I'd really like that," I agree, then whisper, "I love you, Mom. Always."

"I love you too, baby, and I promise I'll keep it together from now on. Sleep well."

"You too." I hang up and inhale deeply before I turn around. When my eyes catch Gaston's, which are filled with concern, the promise I made to my mom about never trusting a man feels like a thousand-pound weight on my shoulders.

"Everything okay?"

I want to say no and tell him everything—every sad detail about my parents and their marriage. I want to tell him about my dad and how close we used to be, about how I don't even hear from him anymore. As much as I want to tell him all of that, we're not at a point where I would feel comfortable unloading that kind of baggage on him, and honestly, I'm still not sure he's who he seems to be.

"Yeah, just family stuff."

"You sure? That sounded pretty intense."

"I'm sure you understand better than most people how crazy family stuff can be."

"Yeah," he agrees softly, studying me and still looking concerned, which kills because it makes me like him that much more. "Do you want me to go?"

No, I want to say, but I ignore that urge. I need time to think, time to figure out what I'm feeling. So instead I say, "I'm sorry. It's late, and I have to be up early."

He nods in understanding, and my insides twist with disappointment, but I ignore that feeling too and head toward the door. Without looking, I know he's following, and once I open the door I keep my eyes on my feet, because I won't be able to stomach another of his worried looks.

"Thank you for dinner; it was delicious."

Without warning, he wraps his warm, strong hand around the side of my neck, and his fingers apply pressure to my chin, forcing my eyes up to meet his. "Why do I get the feeling that this isn't just goodbye, but *goodbye*?"

My jaw aches as I fight to keep an unexpected wave of tears at bay. I don't know anyone else who can read me so easily, and it really sucks that he seems to be able to, even after knowing me such a short time. "I think the fact you're leaving means *goodbye* is the correct word to say."

"Don't try to be cute. You know exactly what I'm saying," he growls, and my pulse speeds up. I attempt to pull away from his grasp, but he doesn't loosen his hold. Instead, his fingers tighten; then his other hand grips my hip firmly, keeping me in place and anchoring me to him as his eyes bore into mine. "No. No fucking way am I going to allow you to tangle me in your web that smells like cupcakes and frosting and then just walk away without knowing if I'll see you again."

"I'm not trying to tangle you in my web," I deny shakily.

"You didn't have to try. I got caught all on my own." His thumb skims my jaw. "I don't want to be free, but this isn't just about me, sweetheart. I need to know you want me where I am."

I block him out the only way I can. I close my eyes, needing just a few seconds to wrap my mind around what he's saying. I can still hear my mom's plea in the back of my mind, but the feeling inside my chest—the one telling me to take a chance on this guy who puts me at ease, turns me on, and makes me laugh—is louder.

"You'll see me again," I tell him quietly while opening my eyes.

"When?"

"Whenever you have time," I say, figuring he has a business to run, so it should be a few days before I see him again. And hopefully by then, I'll have talked to Leah, and she'll have helped me sort through my emotions.

"Tomorrow?"

Crap. So much for my plan. Then again, maybe not. "I'm having dinner with my mom tomorrow." I use the only lifeline I have.

"Come to my place after."

"I . . ." I start to tell him it might be late and that I will most likely be too tired to drive anywhere.

"Did I forget to mention I live in this building?"

"What?" I stare at him with wide eyes.

"I'm ten floors above you. After you have dinner with your mom, come up. We'll talk and hang out for a while before I leave for work."

"You live in this building?" I'm shocked, and my voice reflects that. "Yeah."

"But I've never seen you before."

He smirks, pressing his forehead to mine. "Sweetheart, thousands of people live here. I'm just one of those thousands."

He's right, but you'd think I would have noticed him at some point—especially since he's so obviously . . . noticeable. "I guess you're right," I say, and he smirks again.

"Now tell me I'll see you tomorrow night."

"You're relentless." I sigh, trying to sound put out, when I actually feel kind of elated he's so set on spending time with me.

"You're right, especially when I see something I want. Now make this easy on yourself and tell me what I want to hear."

A shiver slides up my spine, and my voice is breathy when I give him the response he wants. "You'll see me tomorrow night."

"Good." His thumb tugs down on my chin ever so slightly; then his lips press against mine. When his tongue touches the inner edge of my bottom lip, I lean in, and he groans before he releases me. "Get some sleep. I'll see you tomorrow night." Feeling a little off balance from the kiss and his sudden pulling away, I nod. He grins, and my knees actually shake. "Night, sweetheart."

"Night," I tell his back as he turns to leave.

As soon as he passes the threshold, I shut the door and lock the three locks. I'm pretty sure I hear him laughing through the door. It would be embarrassing if he knew just how much he affects me. I go to the kitchen and grab my empty wineglass and pour the rest of the bottle into it as I look around. The kitchen is spotless. Surprisingly, he didn't just cook; he cleaned as he went, so after we both ate, only the pans, our plates, and the silverware were left to place in the dishwasher, and he did that too before starting it.

With a slight shake of my head and a smile on my lips that I can't control, I take my wine with me to the living room and turn out the lights there, leaving only the moonlight outside to help guide me to my bedroom.

I flip on my bedroom light and then get undressed, tossing my clothes toward the hamper, not even checking to see if they make it in. Sipping wine, I go through my normal routine. I take off my makeup, put on my nightly face mask, and start up the bath, even though I already had a shower.

Since I can remember, I've taken a bath every night except when I was away at school—because first, I shared a bathroom with three other girls, and second, the bathtub was just big enough to stand in. But as soon as I moved back home, my routine fell right back into place, and every night like clockwork, I soak in the tub and let the warm water and my magical bath salts erase the day. After the bath is full, I drop in two scoops of my lavender vanilla bath salts and climb in with my glass of wine.

Between the hot water and the alcohol, by the time I get out and dried off, I'm completely relaxed. I don't bother getting dressed like normal; I shut off the light and drop face-first into my bed, falling asleep even before I have time to overthink dinner with Mom and spending time with Gaston tomorrow night.

Suggestion 5

Open Up a Little and See What Happens

Chrissie

I flip the sign on the door to my shop to CLOSED and then scan the space, checking to make sure all the lights are off before I step outside to lock up. I lace my keys in my hand, turning them into a weapon out of habit. It's a move I was taught during a self-defense class my dad forced me to take before I left for New York. Not that it's necessary here. Crime is almost nonexistent in this area. The streets are well lit, and even now, there are lots of people around. Some are shopping at small boutiques, while others are at the restaurants and bars that line the block.

I walk down the sidewalk toward my car, feeling like I always do after a long day—completely and utterly exhausted. I really should look into hiring someone full time to either open the shop in the mornings or to close it in the evenings, but I'm just always too worried about my bottom line to bite that bullet.

Things at the Sweet Spot have been good, really good. My business is growing steadily, and I'm constantly getting new customers. But the minuscule line between being in the black versus in the red could change at the drop of a hat, and that line makes me uneasy.

With a tired sigh, I get into my car, program the restaurant I'm meeting my mom at into my GPS, and take off toward my destination. Ten minutes into the fifteen-minute drive, I stop at a red light and yawn for the third time in a row. If I'm going to make it through dinner and then see Gaston tonight, I'm going to have to break one of my rules and have a Coke with dinner.

I spot my mom sitting on one of the benches just outside the door of the restaurant when I arrive, and she waves when she sees me. I wave back, then search the almost-full lot for a place to park and by a miracle manage to find a spot. As soon as I get out of my car, my mom greets me with a hug, and like always, the moment her arms wrap around me, my entire body relaxes. Even at my age, I can't deny the healing power of one of my mom's hugs.

"I've missed you," she tells me as she tightens her arms around me.

"It's been a week, Mom." I sigh like a put-out teenager without loosening my hold or letting her go.

She laughs, then leans back enough to look at my face. "You look tired."

"Thanks." I roll my eyes.

"You're still beautiful, honey. You just look like you haven't slept much."

I can't say the same about her. Even with everything that has happened, she is beautiful, with hardly any wrinkles, thanks to the facial routine she passed down to me. She has dark-auburn hair that's still shiny and full and a body that's trim because of yoga and swimming five days a week. She didn't let herself go after being married and having kids, which makes me wonder why my dad felt the need to stray. I've never met the woman he married—haven't even looked her up on social media—and I don't know that I want to. Still, a part of me is curious about her. A part of me wants to understand what happened and to see who he left my mom for after so many years of seeming happy.

"Can we go eat and not talk about how tired I look?"

"Absolutely." She takes my hand and leads me toward the restaurant.

The place is busy, but thankfully there are still a few tables available. We're seated immediately, and right away I order a Coke, while my mom orders water. Since we both know what we want to eat after looking at the menu briefly, we give the waitress our dinner orders as well, and she tells us she'll be right back with our drinks before she walks away.

"You never drink soda this late," she says, unrolling her utensils and placing her napkin in her lap.

"I have some paperwork to do tonight," I lie. "I need the kick if I'm going to make it through that." After our conversation last night, I'm not sure how she'd react to Gaston, and really, I don't think I want to find out.

"You're always working too hard." She says the same thing she always does when I'm talking about work, then shakes her head and holds out her hand. "All right, hand over your phone so I can see how beautiful Leah looked."

"You know, if you got a better phone, you could have seen all the pictures over text while I was away."

"Like I've told you and your brother, I don't need a new phone. The one I have does exactly what I need it to do—make calls. I don't want to become one of those people who's constantly looking at their phone."

"Whatever. I'll talk to Chris. Your birthday is coming up, so maybe we will just buy you one."

"Give me your phone," she orders. I click my photo icon, then hand my phone over, and I watch as her expression changes while she slides through each photo. "I wish I could have been there," she tells me, studying the screen.

"Me too."

She was, of course, invited to the ceremony, but she also knew that if she went, no one would have been able to take care of the shop while I was away. Yes, I love Aubrey and Rachelle and know they are more than capable of handling things in my absence, but they are also just kids who are still in high school. This is just one more reason I need to hire someone. My mom should have been able to go with me to Tennessee instead of covering for me in my absence.

"I think I need to really start looking for someone to hire full time at the shop to help me out," I say, and my mom instantly drops my phone on the table and pins me in place with her gaze.

"I think that would be smart," she agrees, then continues with an understanding look in her eyes. "I know you love what you do, but you need a life, honey—something that doesn't involve cookies, cakes, and getting up early every day."

"It's my dream," I reply, feeling a little defensive. My friends and family are always complaining that I work too much, that I never have time for them. And they're right, but I want my shop to be successful. I want my mom and even my dad to know the money they invested in my future and the sacrifices they made were worth it.

"Yes, but . . ." She pauses, pressing her lips together, and a sad light fills her eyes. "The Sweet Spot was never your only dream. You used to talk about wanting a family—a husband and kids." Before I can tell her I'm okay, that having even one part of my dream come true gives me contentment and happiness, she continues, and I brace. "I'm so sorry about last night."

"Mom, it's okay."

"It isn't. I shouldn't have called you. I really shouldn't have asked you to make me that stupid promise." She looks away. "That's not what I want for you. I want you to find someone to fall in love with." She meets my gaze once more. "I want to see you happy, and one day, I want to chase my grandchildren—who are sure to be hellions—all over the place when they come to visit. I know I haven't been acting like it, but I do still believe in love. And I know in my heart you'll find it." She pulls in a breath. "Heck, maybe even I'll find it again." Relief and hope fill me at once.

I take a deep breath as we look each other in the eye. I can't imagine what she's going through or the pain she's felt since my dad walked away from her. I feel a little of it myself every time I think about him, but I will never understand the true depth of her despair. It wasn't me who planned my entire future around him. It wasn't me who was counting on him being there to spend the rest of my life with after my brother and I grew up and moved out. And I for sure didn't experience him saying he was in love with someone else before having to endure the humiliation of him marrying someone else before the ink was even dry on the divorce papers.

"You'll find happiness again, Mom. Whether it's with a man or just yourself, you'll find it again."

"I know." She looks away briefly to hide the tears I see forming in her eyes. Once she's pulled herself together, she turns her head toward me, and her gaze is now filled with hope. "After our conversation last night, I realized I need to start focusing on me and the things I've always wanted to do—things that will make me happy." She smiles, but I can tell it's forced. "I can go to Hawaii, on a cruise, or around the world alone. I don't need someone with me to do those things."

"You don't," I agree.

"I don't." She lifts her chin. "But if I happen to stumble across someone in Hawaii or on a cruise, I might just take him along for my next adventure."

I laugh, and soon she's laughing with me. I can't remember the last time we laughed together. It's been too long. "I hope you find that man, Mom," I tell her.

"Me too, honey, but even if I don't, I'll find a way to be happy again. I'm determined."

"Good," I whisper through the tightness in my throat.

"I want the same for you, you know."

"What?" I ask, a little caught off guard by her suddenly serious tone.

"I want you to be happy too," she tells me softly.

"I am happy, Mom," I assure her.

She shakes her head. "I know you think you are, honey, but I promise you, when you actually feel happiness, the kind of happiness that roots itself in you and takes over your soul, you'll know what I mean when I say I want you to be happy."

I understand what she's saying. I also know I'll never be able to convince her that I am actually happy. *Kind of . . . pretty much.* Luckily for me, our drinks and then dinner arrive, giving us something else to focus on. We both dig into our meals with abandon and chat only about things that are easy to talk about.

After we finish with dinner, we walk out to the parking lot and hug goodbye before we get into our cars. As I drive to my place, the anticipation of seeing Gaston causes a jolt of adrenaline to sweep through my system. I should have opened up to my mom about him tonight. She was her old self throughout dinner, and I know the woman she was before my dad did what he did would have been happy to hear about the guy I was seeing.

Maybe next time, I think as I park in my designated parking spot. I send Gaston a text when I get out of my car to let him know I'll be there soon, and he immediately texts back with a smiley emoji. When I got up this morning, I found two texts from him: one from last night wishing me a good night and the other from this morning wishing me a good morning. Having been with guys who didn't put themselves out there, I wasn't sure what to think about Gaston's texts. Really, I'm not sure what to think about him in general. He doesn't seem to be playing any sort of game. If anything, he just seems sure about wanting to get to know me.

Once I reach the lobby, I check my mailbox. I shove the stack of what I'm sure is mostly junk mail into my purse, then walk toward the bank of elevators. Inside, I scan the numbers, looking for the one that will take me up to Gaston. I never paid much attention to the numbers before now, but when I see that his is actually the last on the keypad, my heart lodges in my throat.

The top-floor condos are all huge, at a little over three thousand square feet. All have balconies triple the size of mine, along with three bedrooms, four baths, and designer kitchens. When I bought my place, I was shown one of the units, even though it was way more than anything I could afford. I remember walking through the door, wondering why someone would pay so much to live in a building when they could buy a house on the beach for not much more. I should say, I wondered *until* I saw exactly how luxurious they were.

I press the button, and as soon as the doors close, my nerves kick into overdrive. It doesn't take long to reach the top floor, and when the doors open, I find him waiting for me, leaning back against the wall with his hands shoved in the front pockets of his jeans. We stare at each other, and then after a long moment, he holds out his hand and grins.

I place my hand in his and then laugh as he tugs me toward him and wraps me in a hug. Apparently, my mom isn't the only one with magical hugs. As soon as I'm pressed against him, I let out a quiet sigh.

"You smell like cake," he tells me, burying his face in my hair.

"Is that a bad thing?"

"Hell no, I fucking love cake."

Giggling, I look up at him. He studies my face for a moment, and my entire being starts to fill with anticipation. When he leans in and only softly touches his lips to the tip of my nose, I'm disappointed, but just slightly, because that kiss was sweet.

"Come on. I want to show you my place," he says, and I let him take my hand and lead me down the hall.

The space, even from my vantage point near the entrance, is beautiful. In the sunken living room, there is an overstuffed light-gray couch, two darker-gray chairs, and a long, shiny, black coffee table, all centered around a fireplace that takes up part of the wall, with the biggest TV I have ever seen mounted above it. I can see the kitchen, at least part of it, and it's all dark cabinets and marble countertops. The entire space looks like it's staged to go on the market tomorrow, not like someone is actually living in it.

I start to tell him his home is beautiful but stop when a tiny white blur flies across the room. I freeze for a moment, thinking I'm imagining things, and then blink in surprise when Gaston bends down to pick up the fluffy ball of white fur.

"You have a dog," I say, and he grins, running his fingers over the top of the dog's head as it attempts to lick the underside of his jaw.

"This is LeFou," he tells me, coming closer to where I'm standing.

"You're kidding? You named your dog LeFou—LeFou, as in Gaston's sidekick from *Beauty and the Beast*?"

"I didn't name him. My mom did before she delivered him to me as a birthday present. At that point, I couldn't change his name, since he wouldn't respond to anything else." I start to laugh, the image of him with the tiny dog and its name too much for me to handle. "You're going to give him a complex," he tells me, and I laugh harder, then wipe away the tears that are running down my cheeks.

"Sorry, LeFou, you're adorable." I hold out my hand, and he sniffs my fingers before he licks them. I carefully take the tiny dog from his grasp, and the moment I have him in my hold, he goes crazy, licking any part of me he can reach while his tiny body wiggles uncontrollably. "He's cute. And your place is beautiful," I tell Gaston, and his expression fills with pride.

"You haven't seen the best part yet." He places his hand against my lower back and leads me down the steps, into the living room, and toward the kitchen. He stops us at the edge of the island and asks, "Would you like a glass of wine or something else?"

"I'll have wine," I tell him, rubbing the top of LeFou's head.

He lifts his chin toward his dog. "Put him down, sweetheart, and get comfortable while I get us a drink."

Without a word, I set LeFou on the ground, then watch as he runs around the island and into the kitchen, where Gaston is now holding a treat. Once LeFou has the small dog cookie in his mouth, he takes off at a run, disappearing into the living room.

I remove my purse from my shoulder and pull out a pastry bag I brought with me. I set it on the marble countertop, then slip off my jacket and place both my purse and coat on one of the five unique wooden barstools that line the island. When I finish with my task, I look into the kitchen and notice he's standing in the middle of the big, open space, holding a bottle of wine, but his eyes—with a somewhat surprised look in them—are on the paper bag. That look shifts to satisfaction when his gaze lifts to meet mine.

"What?"

"You brought me oatmeal raisin cookies, didn't you?"

"No," I deny with a shake of my head. "I brought oatmeal raisin cookies with me."

"Liar." He sets down the bottle of wine, then starts to prowl toward me. The look in his eyes is predatory, and I take a step back, and then he reaches out to capture my hip with his hand. "Admit it: you brought me cookies." His deep, velvety voice hypnotizes me, and I nod in silent agreement. "Sweetheart, you do know I gotta kiss you now, right?"

My lips part in surprise from his words and from the feel of his hand as he tangles his fingers into my hair. My eyes slide closed as he tilts my head, and then my heart stops when his lips touch mine, and a whimper I can't control slides up my throat when his tongue licks across the seam of my mouth. I open for him, and the kiss deepens, our tongues tangling together, and I latch on to his waist, digging my nails into his sides and feeling nothing but hard muscle under my hands.

He growls, and the vibration of that sound seeps through my skin and settles between my thighs. My mind goes dizzy with desire, and my body begins to buzz with need. I've never been kissed like this. I feel the possessive brand of his mouth on mine and his hold, like he's staking his claim, telling me without words I belong to him. My fingers dig into his flesh, and I groan into his mouth as he slows the kiss and pulls away. When I blink my eyes open, he touches his lips to mine one last time.

I stare into his eyes, which I'm sure match my own with need. "Um . . ." I clear my throat, then say stupidly, "You must really like my cookies."

His head drops back to his shoulders as he laughs loudly, and then he wraps his arms around me and drops his chin to the top of my head, giving me a tight squeeze. "Yeah, I really fucking like your cookies."

"Duly noted," I whisper, feeling his body start to shake with silent laughter before the sound erupts from his chest once more. I've never been held by a man when he's laughing, but I have to admit—I like it a lot.

When he finally gets over the hilarity of my apparent dorkiness, he leans back to look at me. Once more, I'm mesmerized by the look he's giving me, which means I'm caught off guard when he brushes his mouth over mine and lets me go.

"Let's get you a drink."

I don't tell him that I don't need a drink; I already feel lightheaded and giddy, like I've drunk a bottle of wine just from his kiss. As he seems prone to do, he grabs my hand and leads me with him deeper into the kitchen, where he pours a glass of wine for me, then grabs a beer from a small fridge under the counter for himself. He hands me the glass and then places his hand in the middle of my back, urging me toward his balcony. Having been outside earlier, I know it's cold, so I brace as he slides the glass open. Surprisingly, warmth radiates toward me, and I follow him out. I seek out the source of the heat warming my skin and notice that there are three outdoor heaters positioned at the top of the ceiling and angled down toward the comfortable-looking couch that is situated against the building.

"This is why I bought this place," he tells me while moving closer to the edge of the balcony. "Looking out at the ocean from this spot made me feel like I was home in New Jersey."

I take in the view. Just like from my place, there is nothing but sand and ocean with the moon and stars shining down on it, making it look like a piece of art. Something someone years ago would have painted that today would be sold for millions of dollars.

"It's a great view, but I have to admit—I never want to see your electric bill, and I really don't want to be here when the environmental and global warming experts show up and start picketing outside the building." I smile while glancing at him from the corner of my eye.

He laughs, then wraps one hand around my waist and leans over, touching his lips to the top of my head. "You're safe from the environmentalists. This is the first time I've turned the heaters on since I moved in, and I did it about two minutes after you told me you were here."

"Good to know you're taking global warming seriously."

"Just trying to do my part. I should also mention, in case the powers that be are listening, I also recycle and use reusable shopping bags."

"Now you're just showing off," I say through my laughter, and he chuckles quietly.

Starting to get cold from the breeze coming off the sea, even with his warmth seeping into my side, I step away from him and go to the couch and take a seat, and he does the same, settling right next to me.

"How was dinner with your mom?" he questions, placing his arm around my shoulders and bringing me closer to him.

Normally, I would not be okay with a guy being so touchy, but there is something about the way he does it that makes it feel right.

"It was good." I peek up at him, thinking it's a good thing he was so adamant last night about seeing me again. Who knows what would have happened if he'd just walked out of my apartment after my phone call with my mom? I don't know if I would've had the courage to reach out to him, even if I'd wanted to, because if the shoe was on the other foot, I would have told him to jump in a lake. "My parents divorced about a year ago," I say, wondering where those words are coming from. I didn't plan on telling him that.

"I'm sorry."

"Me too." I chew on the inside of my cheek.

"Is that what the phone call was about last night?"

"Yeah." I toy with the stem of my wineglass while focusing on the view. "My mom . . . well, really, none of us saw it coming. We definitely didn't see any signs that he'd been having an affair for a while and wanted to marry his mistress." His arm, which is around my shoulders, tightens briefly before he begins to smooth his thumb up and down along my arm, like he's silently encouraging me to continue. "My mom has not been herself since then, but I think last night was her breaking point."

"What happened?" he asks gently, never stopping the comforting sweeping movement of his thumb along my arm.

"She found out my dad's taking his new wife to Hawaii, a place my mom always wanted to travel to with him." I look at him, and his head tips down toward mine. "I think she realized what she was missing, not in my dad but in their marriage. Both my parents sacrificed a lot for my brother and me, and I wonder if part of that was the relationship they had with each other. I mean, I don't know, but I think they got so lost in being parents to the two of us that they forgot why they were together. Or that's what I think, anyways."

"I get losing your way after having kids, sweetheart, but the cheating I absolutely do not understand."

"I don't get that part either," I say, taking a sip of wine. "I would've never thought my dad would have an affair. Not when he always made it clear that his family was important to him."

"Was?"

I know what he's asking, so I answer, "I haven't spoken to him since I found out about his mistress, and he hasn't attempted to get in touch with me. My brother, Chris, hasn't heard from our dad either. He's completely cut us out of his life. The only reason I even know he's still alive is because he and my mom have mutual friends that keep her updated on what he's doing."

"Jesus, that's fucked up." He takes a pull from his beer, then looks at me. "I'm sorry to say this, baby, but those friends of hers are not helping her heal. If anything, they're making things harder on her. She needs to move on; she doesn't need people giving her updates about your dad."

"You're right," I agree. I've never thought about how those updates are affecting her, but I'm sure they aren't helping her move on with her life. Actually, I'm sure they've been preventing her from moving on at all.

"Tell her that." His thumb stops moving so his fingers can squeeze. "Tell her she needs to make it clear she doesn't want the updates, and if they can't be there for her without bringing him up, she needs to let them go."

"I'll tell her," I whisper through the sudden tightness in my throat and chest.

"It will be easier for her to live her life without knowing what he's doing with his. I told you about my dad being in love with my mom and her not feeling the same. It hurt him every time he had to listen to someone telling him she was seeing someone new." He shakes his head. "It took him a long time to realize that all the time he spent analyzing every detail of her life, trying to find a way to make her see him, was preventing him from finding someone who actually wanted to be with him."

"You're very insightful," I say, and the gorgeous smile he bestows on me nearly makes me skip a breath. "I really do think she's on the right path. Tonight, she told me that she's going to do all the things she always wanted to do, and she even insinuated she's open to finding love again, if she happens to meet the right man."

"She'll find it." He brushes his lips against my forehead, and my eyes slide closed.

I lean farther into him, resting my head against his shoulder and trying to figure out if I should have opened up like I did. But I wonder for only a moment before he proves once more that he can read me, even without looking into my eyes.

"I'm glad you talked to me."

"Me too," I agree quietly, feeling warm and safe in his embrace—something that's odd, considering this is only the fourth time I've been in his presence. We don't talk for a few minutes, and the silence between us feels comfortable. "What time do you have to go to work?"

"I'm the boss, so I can come and go as I please. When you tell me you're tired, I'll take you down and then leave for work. Until then, I'm here with you."

"What time did you get home this morning?" I lean back to catch his eye. His first text came early this morning, even earlier than I got up to get ready for work.

"Close to six."

"You must be exhausted."

"I'm good. I slept most of the day, and really, I never need much more than six hours at a time to feel rested."

"You're lucky. I think I could sleep for a week and still not feel caught up," I admit, resting my head back on his shoulder as the wine I've drunk and the day I've had start to catch up with me.

"When is your day off?"

I snort at his question, and his brows furrow in irritation. "The shop's open seven days a week. I don't have a day off. Well, I do have a half day Sundays, since I open at seven and close at noon."

"Babe, that's not healthy."

"You're probably right, but I also love what I do, so I don't mind working so much."

"I get that, but you also need time for yourself. You can't work all the time. What do you do for fun?"

"Bake."

He shakes his head. "Besides that."

I think about it, trying to come up with one single thing I do for fun, and then realize I've got nothing. The last time I went out was for Leah's bachelorette party, and before that it had been months. Prior to opening the Sweet Spot, I used to take pottery classes, go to book club meetings, swim a few days a week, and join my mom for yoga from time to time. Now all I do is work and sleep.

"I really need to hire someone full time to help out at the shop." I sigh.

"Is your business stable enough to take on someone full time?"

"Yeah, I just get jittery when I think about doing it."

"You're smart. Taking a financial risk when you own your own business isn't something you should do unless you have weighed the pros and cons. Do you have an accountant?"

"No, I've always done my own books."

"Seriously?"

"I don't have a lot of overhead, so there isn't much to manage."

"If you want, I can put you in contact with my accountant. I'm sure you're doing a great job, but Josh might be able to look over your books and tell you if he thinks it would be a good idea to hire someone right now. Sometimes a second opinion will help put your mind at ease and give you the push you need."

"I'd really appreciate that," I say, right before I suddenly cover my mouth to yawn. "Sorry, wine always makes me a little sleepy. I should have thought about that."

"Don't apologize. You need to go to bed." He gets up, then pulls me up to stand in front of him, brushing his lips over my forehead before going to an electric box on the wall to turn off the heaters. I pick up his empty beer bottle and grab my glass, taking them to the kitchen. Not wanting to snoop to find the trash, I leave the bottle on the counter but drop my glass in his dishwasher.

When he comes inside, he tells me he'll be right back before his broad shoulders disappear around a corner just off the kitchen. I pick up LeFou when he appears at my feet and cuddle him against my chest as I take the moment alone to explore Gaston's living room.

There are only a few photos on the stand below the TV, and I assume the one with him and a beautiful older woman who's smiling hugely at the camera while he laughs down at her is Gaston and his mom. In another photo a man—most likely his dad, since they look alike—is surrounded by three beautiful women, and the youngest two are kissing his cheeks. The other woman, who's obviously their mom, has her arms wrapped around his neck from behind and her chin resting on the top of his head, smiling softly. I can tell by the look in his dad's eyes that he was happy, he was loved, he was living his best life, and there was nowhere he'd rather be than with his family. I'm glad he got to experience that kind of happiness and love before he passed away. The last photo is a shot of an old woman who's standing at a stove, stirring something in a pot that looks almost as big as her. Her gray hair is up in a tight bun, and her plump body is encased in a formfitting green dress with a white apron tied around her waist.

I stare at that photo the longest, because I can't count the number of times I've seen my own grandmother in that exact position. Anytime I went to visit her, she was in the kitchen, cooking something or baking some kind of sweet treat. She was the best; she never complained when

I wanted to help. Instead, she'd smile and tell me to get my stool, and then she'd give me a job, and I'd work along with her. I know if she were alive today, she'd be in my shop helping me, and I would love every second of having her around. Actually, I'd relish it.

I finish my perusal of the living room, and just when I'm heading back toward the kitchen with LeFou still in my arms, Gaston reappears. He's no longer wearing the jeans he had on but has changed into navy-blue slacks that show off his amazing thighs and a fitted button-down shirt that's tucked in, emphasizing his muscular torso. He has a fancy belt around his hips and shiny shoes on his large feet. He looks every bit the businessman he is. He also looks way too gorgeous and seriously out of my league.

Our eyes lock from across the room, and I stand in place, stuck in some kind of trance. He comes toward me, taking his dog from my arms and placing him on the ground.

"I should wait to kiss you good night until after I've walked you to your door, but I'm feeling a little greedy," he tells me, and my breath catches as he once again palms the back of my head and lowers his mouth to mine. The kiss is just as hot as the one we shared earlier—maybe even hotter, which seems impossible. I melt into him, and my lips part, allowing him to sweep his tongue across mine. He tastes like mint and beer—a combination that is uniquely him.

The kiss deepens, and I cling to him so I don't fall on my face. When he slowly pulls away, I'm in such a daze I don't even think as he grabs my bag and coat. I just follow him out of his apartment with my hand held firmly in his and get into the elevator.

When we reach my floor, he hands me my purse, and even as I find my keys and unlock the door to my place, my mind is still buzzing, which means I can hardly remember my name when he kisses me again. As he pulls away once more, he promises to see me tomorrow before handing me my coat with a cocky grin, telling me softly to lock up before leaving, and then closing the door as he goes.

I stare at the closed door with my bag and coat in my hand, and my heart beats wildly in my chest. Still drunk on his kiss, I know I really need to talk to Leah. At this point, I don't care that she's away on her honeymoon. Tomorrow, I'm going to call her.

With that thought in my head, I walk into my living room, drop my stuff on the chair, and then go to my bedroom to strip out of my clothes. I don't take a bath; I just crawl into bed, where I think of Gaston, his kindness, his cute little dog, and the way he makes me feel before I fall asleep.

Suggestion 6

FIND YOUR HAPPINESS

CHRISSIE

With a cup of coffee in one hand, I open the fridge to try to figure out what to make myself for breakfast. Unlike my bakery, which is always stocked with everything I could possibly need, my fridge at home is mostly empty. I have a carton of egg whites, a few pieces of turkey, and some cheese. With no other options, I decide on an egg white omelet, making a mental note to stop at the grocery store after I close down the shop tonight.

I take a sip of coffee, then set down my coffee cup and grab a pan to place on the stovetop to warm up. Just as I start to pour the egg whites into the now-hot pan, there is a knock at the door, and a sudden thrill runs down my spine.

I touch my wet hair and glance down at my short kimono-style robe, under which I'm wearing nothing, then look toward the door, debating what to do. I can guess who it is, since no one ever stops by without calling, especially not this early. There's only one person I know who'd have a reason to be up right now.

Three more knocks come in a row, so I tighten the belt around my waist and try to calm my suddenly pounding heart. I check the peephole and swallow hard as I unlatch the locks and let Gaston in.

My focus zeroes in on the two paper coffee cups and the brown paper bag he's carrying, and the scent from the bag makes my stomach grumble. It smells delicious, like eggs, bacon, and fresh-baked pastries. If he brought me food, I might just ask him to marry me.

"Sorry, I'm not dressed yet," I say, but his eyes aren't anywhere near my face. No, they're riveted on my robe and legs—mostly my legs. "Um, I'm just going to put something on." My cheeks feel warm as his gaze slowly wanders up my body and then over my face and wet hair.

"You're stunning, seriously fucking stunning, sweetheart."

"Thanks." I bite the inside of my cheek. His dark eyes track up and down me once more, causing my nipples to pebble and my core to tighten. I don't think I've ever had a man look at me with so much desire; it's a heady feeling.

"Please don't rush to get dressed on my behalf."

I'm pretty sure that if I don't put something on and he keeps looking at me like he is, I'm going to jump him, and I don't think that would be a very good idea, so I say, "I'll be back. Make yourself comfortable." I rush for my bedroom, then skid to a stop when I remember I left the stove on. I make a beeline for the kitchen, turn off the burner, and move the pan into the oven to cool.

I spin around after slamming the oven door shut and crash right into a hard body. A spark of excitement rushes through me as warm hands capture my waist, and without thinking, I lift my hands to his chest, then slide them up to his shoulders—not to push him away, but just to hold on.

"I need to get dressed." I lick my bottom lip, causing his eyes to drop to my mouth, and I shiver when his hands slide farther down my back, pulling me closer against his muscular torso.

"Why's that?" he asks, his voice husky. The deep, growly sound and the feel of the silky material of my kimono sliding up the backs of my thighs and bottom as he bunches it in his fists make me instantly wet.

"I don't have panties on," I whisper, and he groans, brushing his lips softly over the top of mine before moving them to my neck. "I don't think it's very appropriate for me to be walking around my kitchen with you here without anything on under this scrap of material."

"Are you trying to drive me mad?" he asks, nipping the shell of my ear with his teeth.

"I think I should be asking you that question." I get up on my tiptoes when he nips the lobe again, making me whimper. I press my breasts against his chest, and his warm lips dance from my ear and across my neck, and his hot hands pull up the bottom of my robe so he can grab hold of my ass cheeks in each of his big palms. Panting and beyond turned on, I moan when his fingers slide down the crease to find my wetness from behind.

"Christ, you're soaked," he hisses, and then suddenly I'm no longer standing but up off the ground, being placed on the edge of the counter. He pushes my knees apart to stand between them, then leans into me, both his hands on either side of my hips, caging me. I tip my head to the side as he slants his in the other direction. The moment my lips part, he slides his tongue into my mouth, and I kiss him back with wild abandon.

I cling to him until he slows the kiss and pulls out of my grasp. "Stay just like this, sweetheart. I'll be right back."

"What?" I ask in a daze, breathing heavy, with my heart pounding hard.

"I'm going to eat breakfast. I'll be back in a minute." He kisses me swiftly, then drops to his knees.

My eyes widen in surprise, and then my head falls back to my shoulders as he spreads me open with his fingers and licks up my center. His talented mouth, tongue, and teeth suck, lick, and nip every inch of my pussy until I'm on the verge of crying from pleasure I've never experienced before. I thread my fingers through his hair, and he thrusts two fingers inside me, causing my back to arch and my core to clench tight.

When he wraps his lips around my clit and sucks, I scream his name as I start to come, seeing stars dance behind my closed eyelids. Blood rushes to my head, making me feel dizzy, and I fall back to the counter. As I come down from the high of my orgasm, I feel his lips touch my inner thigh, and I open my eyes to watch him grab the tie to my robe and pull it open.

Exposed to him, I soak up the look in his eyes, feeling drunk on it. My heart starts to pound with a new kind of anticipation when he begins to unbutton his shirt, and my mouth waters when I see his well-defined torso and abs. He drops the shirt to the floor, and I drop my eyes to his cock, which I can tell is huge even behind the zipper of his slacks. He then looms over me and palms both my breasts, making my breath catch. I writhe under his talented mouth and hands as he sucks and pinches my nipples, never giving me a moment to adjust before he moves and changes his angle, keeping me wanting more, guessing what he will do next.

"Please, I need you inside me." I hold myself up with one hand and use my other to grab hold of his jaw and his attention. His heated eyes focus on mine before he bends forward, taking my mouth in another fiery kiss before he pulls away. I start to reach for him but stop when he pulls out his wallet from his back pocket, flips it open, and takes out a shiny silver packet, dropping the wallet to the counter. My chest heaves with excitement, and I fumble with his belt and zipper as he tears open the condom wrapper with his teeth.

"Pull me out, baby," he orders.

I don't hesitate; I wrap my hand around his cock, noticing that my fingertips don't even touch as I free him from his boxers. I stroke him once, thinking that even his cock is beautiful, before he moves my hand away to slide on the condom. When he positions himself at my entrance, I hold my breath, then let it out as he begins to slowly fill me.

"You're so fucking tight—so damn tight. I don't want to hurt you." His jaw tightens, and I know he's trying to be careful, but I don't want careful. I want him inside me. Now.

"You're not going to hurt me." I push up, placing my hands on the counter behind me so we're almost chest to chest, and then I use my heels to pull him closer.

The sound he makes causes my core to flutter around the tip of his cock. "Fuck," he hisses.

"Please," I say, and his eyes meet mine. "I need you."

His eyes flash, and then he fills me full in one smooth thrust. "You okay?"

"God, yes," I whisper, and he pulls back his hips and then sinks back in once more. With my hands still behind me, I watch as he takes me, and I don't think I've ever seen anything more beautiful.

When he slides his hand up my thigh and then uses his thumb to circle my clit, I lose the ability to hold myself up and collapse. I listen to him curse as he brings me closer to orgasm, and I do the only thing I can do. I lift my legs higher, dig my heels in deeper, and hold on to the edge of the counter as he starts to ram into me with hard, brutal thrusts.

My orgasm starts quickly, turning from a pull in my lower belly to my thighs shaking and white splotches dotting my vision. My body bows as I come, and Gaston wraps his hands around the backs of my knees, using them to pull my hips into his over and over.

Still feeling the aftershocks of my orgasm, I listen to him groan and feel his thrusts turn sporadic as he dives over the edge with me. When he plants himself deep inside me, so deep there is no room between us, I raise my legs up higher around his waist to hold on to him. He settles some of his weight against me, covering my body with his, and then he sweetly nuzzles his face in the crook of my neck, breathing heavily.

As my breathing starts to even out, my stomach growls loudly in hunger, and I whisper, "Please tell me you brought me breakfast."

His big body begins to shake with silent laughter, and I feel it everywhere. Between my thighs, where his cock is still buried, against my chest, where his is pressed against mine, and at my neck, where his face is tucked. It's even better than when he was laughing while holding me. The deep sound of his hilarity slowly escapes his mouth and fills the room, and I close my eyes briefly, thinking I could listen to that sound for the rest of my life.

He touches his lips to my neck, then pulls his face from my throat and shoulder, gazing down at me with a soft expression. "I brought you breakfast."

I want to joke and ask him if it's too soon to start designing wedding invitations, but I'm not sure he'd think that's funny. Plus, I really don't relish the idea of him running from my condo, shouting about the crazy wedding-talking woman in 1046. "Thank God. I thought I might have to kill you to get whatever is in that bag you brought in."

He smiles, shaking his head, and then his expression shifts. His eyes leave mine, and he leans back, taking in my exposed skin inch by inch. I watch him watch me as he slowly starts to slide free, and my core contracts in protest, liking him just where he is. I don't even attempt to close my legs, and his eyes flare while his strong jaw clenches.

I can't remember a time I've been more exposed, yet I don't feel self-conscious. All I feel are the delicate threads of desire moving between us, and that makes me feel powerful and adored rather than worried about the slight pooch of my stomach, my full hips, or the hundred other things I don't like about my body.

"I seriously wish I was the kind of man who'd be okay with you lying just like this while an artist painted you, but I know I'd have to kill him for seeing you this way," he tells me while skimming his hands up my thighs and the curve of my waist before stopping to cup both my breasts. His possessive words should not have the effect they do, but there's no denying my nipples pebbling under his palms or the fresh wave of heat that settles between my legs. "You're beautiful."

His gorgeous eyes meet mine, and I melt into a puddle right there on my kitchen counter. He slips his arms around my back and drags me up against him, and once we're face to face, he lowers his head and kisses me softly. He takes his time to explore my mouth while his hands slide my kimono up over my shoulders, then skim down to tie the belt around my waist. Once I'm covered, he kisses me one last time and pulls away, examining my face for a moment before he steps back to drag up his boxers and slacks, zipping the zipper but leaving the button and his belt undone. "I'll be back. I need to go take care of this condom." He brushes his lips over mine, then disappears.

Alone with my thoughts, I wrap my arms around my waist and tip my head back to stare at the ceiling. I didn't plan on having sex with Gaston so soon, but surprisingly, I'm not upset that it happened. There is something about our connection that makes me feel safe and desired. I shake my head, wondering what it is about him that puts me at ease. Normally, this kind of situation would freak me out and I'd be finding an excuse to get up and go to my room right now, hoping the guy would take the hint and leave. For once, I don't want to run, and I for sure don't want him to leave.

"You okay?" I feel a hand on my thigh, and I jump.

"Yeah, I just totally spaced out," I tell him, and he steps back between my legs, then reaches around me to get the coffee, handing me a cup before grabbing the paper bag. I take a sip, surprised it's just how I like it—with lots of hazelnut creamer and extra sugar. "How did you know how I take my coffee?"

He smiles. "I saw your creamer in the fridge when I made dinner, and I notice you have a sweet tooth, so I guessed you'd want extra sugar."

"Wow, that's really observant." I take another sip.

"Have I told you I'm a little obsessed with you?"

"Are you?" My heart pounds, and I wonder if this is actually just a really great dream, because it seems impossible that he's as into me as I am him.

"Oh yeah," he says as he sets his cup next to my hip, then unearths two breakfast sandwiches wrapped in white paper before placing one next to his cup. My stomach growls again loudly, and he smiles as he unwraps a toasted, flaky croissant with eggs, bacon, and cheese peeking from the middle. I take it from him, not caring even a little about the amount of mess I'm about to make as I sink my teeth in. It's delicious, and I can't help the groan of approval my throat makes as I chew.

He grins, and then before he takes a bite from his own sandwich, he asks, "When do you have to leave for work?"

I look around his shoulder to see the clock on the wall across the room as I take another bite. I would normally be leaving in about twenty minutes, but like him, I'm my own boss, so no one is expecting me. And even the baking I need to do this morning can wait. "In about an hour."

"So you have time," he says before taking a sip from his coffee.

"Time for what?"

"A shower."

Him naked in my shower with suds running down his toned physique is something I for sure have time to witness, and even if I don't, I'll make time. I think I might be evicted from the girls' club if I don't. "I think I might be able to fit another shower into my morning schedule."

"Then eat quick, sweetheart, because I'm feeling dirty."

At his words, I take a huge bite of my sandwich, which makes him laugh, and hearing that, I smile around my mouthful. Afterward, I try to focus on eating, but it's hard to do with him moving between toying with the edge of the fabric just beyond my nipple and skimming his fingers up and down my thighs. It probably doesn't help that the ridges and valleys of his abs and the distinct line of hair that disappears into his boxers fascinate me to the point I cannot stop touching them.

I don't know who gives up trying to eat first, but I do know it's me who screams his name as he makes me come in the shower before he groans mine.

I open my shop almost two hours later than I normally do, and for the first time since I opened the Sweet Spot, I don't care that I might have missed out on paying customers. Right now, my mind isn't on work or all the things I need to get done. Instead, it is filled with thoughts of the man who showed up at my house with breakfast and gave me three fantastic orgasms. The guy who made me promise I'd see him when I get home from work, giving me something to look forward to that has nothing to do with my business.

With a smile on my face, I walk through the kitchen to my office and drop off my purse before I grab one of my aprons off a hook near the door. I pull it on over my head and tie it behind my back. Turning on the ovens so they can warm up, I then grab things from the fridge so I can do what I do every morning—make a fresh batch of my chocolate chip cookies. The crispy cookie with diced semidark chocolate might be one of my least-favorite cookies to eat, but they are my best seller. No matter how many I bake a day, I can never seem to keep them in stock.

I spend the morning and afternoon baking and tending to the front of the shop whenever a customer comes in. At 3:30 p.m., Aubrey and Rachelle show up, and like most days when they arrive, they seem to bring the crowd with them. We work in sync, taking orders, boxing things up, and cleaning tables. After five, the flow of customers starts to slow, allowing us to finally take a breath. The girls talk about all the things happening at school, what boy each of them is crushing on this week, and Christmas, which is just a few weeks away.

Normally, I decorate my place from top to bottom for the holiday, but this year, I haven't even bought a Christmas tree for my condo—something I have done every year. Even the shop isn't as festive as it has been the past few years. The girls put out a few decorations, and I paid to have the glass window facing the street painted with a Christmas theme, but that's all.

Last year, the holiday season was seriously depressing. My mom was angry to the point of making the Grinch look like Santa Claus, and my brother didn't come home, leaving me on my own with her. He lives in Maryland with his longtime boyfriend, Sam, and after talking to Mom and reading her vibe, he decided smartly to spend the holidays with Sam's family in Washington, DC. I wanted to jump ship like my brother and go to Leah's parents' home for the day, but it was my mom's first Christmas without my dad.

The day started bad, then ended worse. Mom refused to help me cook, and she barely ate or talked to me, no matter how hard I tried to pull her out of her funk. She spent most of the day (and evening) drinking wine and crying, and then she got sick before eventually passing out. I spent Christmas night keeping an eye on her in a chair next to her bed, which was the crap icing on a really crappy day.

That's why I haven't put much thought into one of my favorite days of the year. I haven't wanted to be excited about it, then feel crushed when I have to witness my mom's depression over a holiday I normally really enjoy. Thinking about my mom now, and hoping she really is going to try to find happiness again, I know I shouldn't let what happened last year determine how I celebrate Christmas this year. I should get a tree, even if it's just a small one. I should also ask my mom what she wants to do this year, since Chris is once again going to Sam's parents' place. He and Sam are planning to fly down here to celebrate the New Year with me and Mom, if she is up to it.

Every year, the city puts on a huge fireworks show at the beach, and I have one of the best views around. Plus, from my place, we don't have to freeze or fight the crowds of people trying to get a good spot. We get to eat, drink, and just enjoy the night before ringing in the New Year and watching the show. I'm sure Gaston will be working, since New Year's is a huge night for every bar and club around, but I'll still invite him to join us. I'll also ask Leah if she and Tyler want to come over.

I like the idea of my best friend and my brother meeting Gaston, even if the idea also makes me a little nervous. I've had a few boyfriends over the years, but I never cared if my family and friends liked them.

Probably because you never saw those relationships going anywhere, a voice in the back of my mind whispers.

"Crap," I hiss, realizing exactly how deep I am with Gaston, even after knowing him only about a week.

"What?" Rachelle asks from where she's restocking a tray of sprinkle cookies in the display case.

"Nothing." I shake my head. "I just remembered something I have to get done today." I give her a reassuring smile.

"I hate when that happens," she says sympathetically. "Is it anything I can help you with?"

"Unfortunately no, honey, but thank you for asking."

"You know I'm happy to help if you need it."

God, she's such a great kid, and I'm really going to miss her and Aubrey when they leave for college.

Aubrey comes out of the kitchen at that moment, carrying a tray of cupcakes, and I look between them, feeling choked up all of a sudden. I still have seven months left with them, but that time is going to fly by. "You know I'm really going to miss you both when you leave me, right?" I say.

"We know," Rachelle whispers, tears forming in her eyes.

"Totally," Aubrey chokes out, and then both of them are rushing toward me with their arms outstretched. We all hug each other, rocking back and forth, and tears start to fill my eyes.

"College is overrated," Rachelle says, making me smile.

"It's also really expensive," Aubrey adds, and I start to laugh as tears track down my cheeks.

"You're going to college, and I promise you'll love every minute of it."

"Yeah, but we'll miss you, and I don't think we'll be able to find a bakery willing to give us free cookies and cupcakes," Aubrey says, stepping back to wipe her cheeks while Rachelle continues to hug me.

"That just means I'll see you both whenever you come home."

"Totally." She nods.

"For sure," Rachelle agrees, giving me one last squeeze before releasing me to swipe her hands down her face.

"We still have a few months, so we should save our tears until then and just enjoy the time we have left," I say, and thankfully they both smile while nodding in agreement. "Good." I smile back. "Now let's finish closing down and go home."

"Are you actually going home when we do, or are you going to stay here baking the rest of the night?" Rachelle asks, planting a hand on her hip while narrowing her eyes at me, and I glance at Aubrey, seeing the same narrowed eyes coming from her. They know my habit of staying late into the night, even if it's just to test a new recipe.

"I'm leaving with you." I hold up the three-finger Girl Scout salute. "I have a couple things to do tonight before I go home."

Aubrey looks at Rachelle, and they share a silent conversation. Rachelle asks, "The guy who came in the other day . . . are you seeing him?"

"Yes." I can't help but smile, and they both let out girly shrieks that make me laugh.

When they're both done squealing in excitement about my new relationship and bombarding me with questions I don't answer, we spend the next hour shutting things down. When we're done, another first happens. I flip the sign to CLOSED and walk to my car, not thinking about the Sweet Spot.

It's crazy how much things have seemed to change since I met Gaston. Is this feeling in my chest what my mom was talking about when she said she wanted me to be soul-deep happy? I'm a little scared yet also excited, which is an odd combination. Not wanting to freak myself out, I focus on getting a Christmas tree, then getting home to spend some time with Gaston.

Suggestion 7

APPRECIATE WHAT YOU HAVE

CHRISSIE

I stand just inside my open front door in nothing but my robe, with Gaston's arms wrapped around my lower back and his mouth on mine. He trails his lips down my neck, stopping to nip my collarbone, and my body responds instantly. My eyes slide closed, and a shiver of desire tickles down my spine. I should be topped off after the night and morning we had, but apparently, like a drug addict, I still need more of him.

Last night, he came down to my place after I got home. When he arrived with LeFou in tow, I was in the middle of trying to get the tree I bought into its complicated stand. So, I distractedly let both of them in, giving LeFou a quick pet before going back to my task. After taking in the situation, Gaston set down his pup and stepped in, taking the stand from me and doing the job himself while asking me questions I answered without thinking. Then he proceeded to make it clear with words and looks that he was annoyed I didn't call to tell him I was stopping to get a tree, and even more annoyed I hauled the somewhat large tree wrapped in twine from my car, into the building, and then up to my condo by myself, when he was just a phone call away.

He got over being annoyed after I apologized and promised to call him next time, but then he got annoyed once more when he asked me where I kept my decorations. I told him they were in my storage unit in the basement of the building. I also told him I'd get them later, because it was getting late and neither of us had eaten. He didn't say anything when I said this; he just gave me another look that stated he wouldn't be happy if I carted the totes upstairs without him.

We ended up bickering about this for a good ten minutes—or I should say, I bickered while holding his pup, and he mostly shook his head like I was adorable and frustrating. I finally gave in when I saw he wasn't going to, and then I grabbed my key for my padlock and took him down to my unit. In the end, he carried my two large red-and-green totes up to my place, only allowing me to carry one small cardboard box that was filled with strings of lights.

I've never had a guy want to take care of me before, even with small things like carrying totes, so his caveman act was sweeter than it was annoying. If I'm honest, I was thankful for his help. It would have taken me forever to get the tree set up, and I would've had to take at least three trips downstairs to the creepy basement without him.

When we got back upstairs, he ordered us dinner from one of the nearby Chinese restaurants while I started to untangle the lights I'd shoved into the cardboard box last year, not knowing my carelessness would come back to haunt me. When he got off the phone, I was sitting on the floor with a knotted ball of lights in my hands, ready to toss the mess into the garbage and buy new ones. Seeing my frustration, he took them from me and had them untangled within minutes. Then he cut the twine from the tree and started to place the lights with ease, even at the top of the tree—something I would've needed a chair to do.

By the time our dinner arrived, we were halfway through one of my boxes of decorations, so we both decided we should finish with the tree first, and when we were done, we didn't eat at the table or on the couch; we both sat on the floor in my living room with only the Christmas lights flickering down at us. We also made love right there, with me straddling his hips before he carried me to bed and finished inside me.

I expected him to leave after that, but he told me he was staying, which meant after we took LeFou out for a walk, I got to experience falling asleep in his arms and him waking me twice during the night to make love to me again.

My alarm went off early, and when it did, he got up with me. While I showered, he went up to his place to grab things to make us breakfast, because I had nothing in my fridge—something he informed me of while I still had shampoo in my hair. I got out of the shower to find him in the kitchen, cooking eggs, bacon, and toast, a meal we ate much like yesterday, me sitting on the counter and him standing between my knees. While we ate, we talked about random things, and then once we both finished, we latched on to each other until I somehow ended up bent over the back of my couch, shouting his name.

I come back to the moment when fingers pinch my nipple and a hand grabs my bottom, pulling me roughly against his erection. I dig my fingers into his strong arms and tilt my head away from his to look into his eyes. "I have to get ready for work."

"In a minute. I'm not done saying goodbye." When his mouth reclaims mine and his tongue slips between my lips, I'm laughing.

It takes some effort on my part, since I don't actually want to stop making out with him, but I find it in myself to pull away. Then I plant my hands against his chest to hold him back. "I want to cook you dinner tonight." My voice is husky, and he smirks, looking pleased with himself.

"Can you cook?"

"I own a bakery, so yes, I know my way around a kitchen."

His arms tighten and he eyes me, looking doubtful. "Babe, baking and cooking are two different things, and I don't want to mention you don't even have any food in your fridge."

"I haven't had time to get to the grocery store." I wave him off. Last night I was going to stop at the store on my way home, but after getting my Christmas tree and seeing the time, I figured I could wait another day. "I'm actually a really great cook."

"What are you going to make?" he questions with a curious smile.

"You'll have to wait and find out," I respond instantly, since I don't actually know what I'm going to make. All I know is it's going to be amazing.

"Now I'm looking forward to tonight more than I was, which seems impossible," he states before he places his lips against mine.

I begin to lose myself in the feelings of desire he seems to bring out of me without trying. Knowing I won't be getting to work at all if things continue, I give his chest a gentle shove, saying, "You need to go, and I need to get ready for work."

"Right," he agrees, seeming as lost as I am. "I'll see you tonight. Call me when you get here."

"Okay." I nod while leaning up on my tiptoes to get one more kiss, but he shakes his head, holding me prisoner while keeping his mouth from mine.

"I mean call me when you reach the parking lot. I'll help you bring up the groceries."

My lips tip up into a smile, and I melt against him, even as I say, "I can carry up a few bags of groceries without your assistance."

"Yeah, but you have a man who's asking you to call him so you don't have to, so work with me."

I have a man. Lord, this is crazy and fast, but I can't even try to deny it feels right. I give in. "I'll call you when I get here."

"Good." He finally gives me the kiss I wanted, then steps back.

I feel tiny paws hit my shins, and I look down at LeFou's white head, then bend to pick him up. "I'll see you tonight, handsome boy." I kiss his furry head, then hand him to his dad. "Have a good day, guys."

"You too, sweetheart. I'll see you later."

"You will," I confirm. I close the door when he turns and starts to walk down the hall, and then I go to my room and get dressed before grabbing my bag and heading to my car. I have a meeting with his accountant scheduled for this afternoon. If he tells me after he looks at my books that I can hire someone full time and still keep my business afloat, then I'm going to put out an ad in the paper and start setting up interviews. I love my shop, but I also really like what is happening between Gaston and me, and I know that if I want it to go somewhere, we're going to need more than just a few stolen hours together.

After I get to work, the day seems to speed by. Gaston's accountant comes in at noon and makes himself comfortable in my office with a few cookies and a cup of coffee. When he emerges an hour later, he tells me it will take him a few days to go over my books more thoroughly, but from what he can see at a glance, I shouldn't be able to hire just one person full time but two if I want. I am a little surprised by this information but nonetheless hopeful.

Not long after he leaves, the girls show up for work. They only stay for two hours, since they have a game to cheer at this evening, so I make the most of the time I have their help. When they leave, I begin the process of shutting things down while tending to customers, and at six on the dot, I close up my shop and head down the block with a recipe for eggplant parmesan tucked in my bag that I'm hoping will prove to Gaston that I can cook.

I park at the grocery store ten minutes later and swing my door open. Just as I start to get out to go into the store, my cell phone, which is in the bottom of my purse, begins to ring. I see Leah's picture on the screen after I dig it out and smile as I answer. "Please tell me you're home."

"I'm home." She laughs, sounding happy and relaxed. "Did you miss me?"

"Yes. And I promise from now on to never take you being available to talk for granted ever again."

"Is everything okay?" She sounds concerned. With her having gone through the last year with me and knowing everything that has happened with my family, her tone isn't surprising.

"Things are better than okay." I smile as I get out of my car and slam the door. "I'm seeing someone."

"What? Where? When? Wh-who?" she stutters on a shout, making me laugh.

"His name is Gaston. Actually, I met him the night of your bachelorette party."

"What?" she yells. "You never said anything about meeting someone, and I'd for sure remember that name."

"I didn't think I'd see him again," I tell her honestly. "Then he sent me flowers before I left for Tennessee and showed up at my shop when I didn't call him while I was out of town for your wedding."

"Wowzers," she breathes. "You've been holding out on me."

"In my defense, you were away enjoying the sun and your new husband."

"True." She laughs. "I'm home now, so tell me everything. I want to know every detail about this guy."

"I will," I say while I grab a shopping cart. "Just not right now. I just got into the grocery store. Plus, I want to hear all about your honeymoon."

"I'll come over tonight and bring dinner along with wine."

As much as I want to see my best friend and catch up, I've been looking forward to seeing Gaston again. Just as I'm about to tell her tomorrow would be better, I hear her husband Tyler's deep voice in the background saying something I can't exactly make out, but it sounds a lot like "No, you won't." I stand in the produce aisle, picking up the things I need with a smile on my face while I listen to the two of them argue. But soon the sounds change to them making out, and I giggle.

"Oh crap," Leah breathes, and my giggles turn into laughter.

"What?" Tyler asks.

The phone is jostled, and Leah comes back to our conversation sounding out of breath. "Can you do dinner tomorrow?"

"Yes."

"My place or yours?" she asks hurriedly.

"Yours. I'll meet you there after I close the shop."

"See you then. Also, I wouldn't be upset if you happen to have a few leftover cupcakes you need to get rid of."

"Got it. Hug Tyler for me, and I'll see you tomorrow."

"Will do." She hangs up, and I do the same.

Just as I start to put my cell in my purse, it rings and Gaston's name flashes on the screen. I answer as it starts to ring for a second time and put it to my ear, saying, "Hey."

"Are you off work?" he asks as I push the cart down another aisle.

"Yeah, I'm at the grocery store near my shop, picking up stuff to wow you with my culinary skills."

"Shit."

"What?" I ask, hearing the frustration in that one word.

"Something went down at the club. I'm heading to get my car now, and I don't know how long it's going to take me to sort shit out. I'm sorry, baby, but I don't think I'll be around for dinner tonight."

As much as I want to see him, I understand. "That's—"

I start to tell him it's okay, but a man pushing a cart who has a petite blonde woman tucked close to his side and under his arm turns the corner at the opposite end of the aisle, catching my attention. They seem locked in a conversation, as if they are the only people in the world. As they come toward me, my body freezes and my tongue gets stuck to the roof of my mouth. I absently hear Gaston call out to me, but my attention is focused on the obviously happy couple headed in my direction.

I don't ever remember my dad smiling like he's doing right now, and I can't recall a time when I ever saw him holding my mom while grocery shopping. Actually, I cannot recall him ever holding her at all.

He's happy, really happy.

Pain slices through my chest, and tears fill my eyes. As quickly as I can, I grab my purse from the seat of the cart and rush out of the aisle, not caring at all about abandoning my shopping cart. I swear I hear someone calling my name, but I just want to get away as fast as I can.

When I reach the parking lot, I unlock my car, get behind the wheel, and start the engine. I try to put the car in reverse to back out of my parking space, but a sob rips from my throat and more tears blind me. With the little bit of sanity I have left, I put my car in park and drop my head to the steering wheel and then lift it quickly when the horn sounds.

A few minutes later, there's a sharp knock on my window, and through my tears I see my father, with the woman who must be his wife standing at his side.

I can't do this. Not now. Maybe not ever.

His voice sounds through the door between us. "Roll down the window." I jerk my head from side to side in silent refusal, causing him to frown. He turns toward the woman like he's seeking advice, and her eyes fill with sympathy as they meet mine. I want to hate her—I *really* want to hate her—but for some stupid reason, I can't seem to drag up that emotion as we stare at each other. My dad knocks on my window again, then tries the handle, and I glare at him.

"We need to talk," he tells me, and anger fills the pit of my stomach.

"Go away."

"Honey," he pleads, and I break right there while sitting in my car, with my father I haven't seen in a year and his new wife watching.

Every ugly emotion I have been tucking away boils to the surface in an instant, and I scream at the top of my lungs, "Just go away! Just leave me alone! I never want to see you again!"

"Chrissie." I hear pain in his voice, but I don't care. He should have called me; he should have talked to me, but he didn't. He's been hiding like a coward for months.

Our staring match is disrupted by a loud roar of pipes that surprises me even inside my car. I turn my head just in time to watch a motorcycle pull up so close to where my father and his wife are standing that they are forced to step back or be run over. My heart pounds as a man dismounts from the black, shining beast between his legs and then rips off the helmet he's wearing. I stare in stunned disbelief at Gaston, and my body instantly begins to relax at the sight of him. I can't make out what he's saying to my father, but my dad glances at me before he nods and takes the woman's hand to lead her away. Gaston stands with his arms crossed over his chest until they get into a car, and he stays like that as they reverse out of their spot. While they're pulling out of the lot, he turns to face me, and his angry expression softens with concern as he comes to my door.

I hit the button for the lock as his hand captures the handle, and a sob rips from my chest as he leans across me to unlatch my belt. He pulls me from my car and into his arms, and I close my eyes as he picks me up.

"Shh, I've got you. You're okay," he tells me, holding me firmly against his warm chest as he walks around the back of my car and places me in the passenger seat to buckle me in.

"You're supposed to be at work." I sniffle, trying to calm myself down.

"Baby, I'm supposed to be here with you." He kisses my forehead, then pulls back to look into my eyes; his fingers touch my cheek, wiping away a few tears. "I need to move my bike, and then I'll get you home."

"Wait. You can't leave your bike here," I say, latching on to him.

"I can, and it won't be here long. I'll have someone pick it up." He removes my hands gently from his shirt, then shuts my door before I can try to convince him I'll be okay to drive home on my own. He parks his bike, and when he's done, he gets in behind the wheel and adjusts the seat to accommodate his long legs.

"Gaston . . ."

"Baby, just relax. We'll talk after I get you home."

"Okay," I agree quietly. Only I don't have a chance to talk to him when I get home, because I fall asleep as soon as he starts driving. I sleep so deeply I don't even wake when he carries me up to his place to put me in his bed.

Suggestion 8

RIDE IN ON YOUR HARLEY AND RESCUE YOUR GIRL

GASTON

I stare at Chrissie's beautiful face for a long time as she sleeps before I finally force myself to move. I might be the boss and am able to come and go as I please, but with three businesses to run and over one hundred employees, I need to check in. I also need to call Luke to let him know I won't be around tonight.

I grab my cell off the bedside table, then head toward the kitchen, with LeFou bouncing at my feet. Luke has been my best friend since childhood, and three years ago, he was the only person I could think of to help me manage things when I decided to expand my business and buy two more bars.

At that time, he was living in New Jersey and working at a warehouse, because even with a master's degree in business management, it was the only job he could find that paid him enough to take care of his wife and daughter. I expected him to have to think about my offer, but he agreed to take the job immediately and packed up his family and moved here within a month. Now I don't know how I would survive without him.

While the cell phone rings, I grab LeFou's food from the pantry and scoop out a cup of his seriously expensive kibble into his bowl.

"Yo," he says. "Everything okay with your girl?"

I called him as soon as Chrissie's phone cut off while she was at the store. I told him what was going down and that I needed him to cover for me. I couldn't be in two places at once, and Chrissie was my priority. As soon as he agreed, I got on my bike and drove like a man on a mission. I wasn't sure what was happening, but whatever it was, it didn't sound good.

I was proven correct when I pulled up next to her car, where a man and woman were standing at her window. When I saw she was crying, a protective instinct I didn't even know I had in me slipped into place. My only concern was making sure she was okay. It took me half a second to figure out the man was her father and the woman was his wife, and when I realized that, I got angry.

I didn't care that her dad was visibly upset or that his wife was too. All I knew was Chrissie was crying, and they were the reason for her tears. When I told them to leave, I expected her father to put up a fight, but he didn't. The only thing that caused me to believe he cared for his daughter even a little bit was the sadness in his eyes as he looked at her before he reached for his wife and guided her to their car.

"Did I lose you?"

At Luke's question, I shake the thoughts from my head. "I'm here," I mutter.

"Is Chrissie okay?"

"She's sleeping. She'll be okay, but I'm not leaving her tonight, so I need you to cover for me and do drawer counts at the club and bars after closing. I also left my bike at Tillie's grocery store on Main and need someone to pick it up for me. Do you still have my spare key?"

"Yeah, I'll send someone to drop Juan off. He knows how to ride a bike, so it'll be all good."

"Thanks, man."

"No problem, but tomorrow you'll need to come in and deal with this order bullshit. I've been on the phone all day with the supplier, and they're adamant that we should've received a full shipment."

"Fuck." This afternoon, before everything went down with Chrissie, I got a call from Georgia informing me that over half the alcohol I ordered was missing, and most of it was top-shelf bottles of liquor. "I'll deal with it tomorrow." I sigh, running my fingers through my hair.

"All right, man. Let me know if you need anything else from me tonight."

"Will do." He hangs up before I do, and I pull my phone from my ear. I call the club and listen to the phone ring.

One of the waitresses answers loudly over the music playing in the background. "Twilight, Hanna speaking."

"Hey, Hanna, it's Gus. Is Georgia around?"

"Yeah, hold on, I'll get her for you." The phone goes silent as I'm put on hold.

Georgia's voice comes on the line. "Gus. Is everything okay?"

"Everything's fine. I just wanted to let you know Luke's gonna be in to handle the drawer counts at the club and bars tonight."

"Are you sick? I can leave and bring you something, or just come over to keep you company." She sounds breathless and hopeful.

"I'm not sick."

"Oh." I hear her disappointment loud and clear.

"Call if there are any issues. I'll have my cell on."

"Okay. See you tomorrow."

"Yeah, later." I hang up.

After I'm done making calls, I wait for LeFou to finish eating, then take him out. Our walk is much shorter than it normally is, and as soon as he takes care of his business, I lead him back inside the building, anxious to return to the woman currently asleep in my bed.

I've never cared about a woman the way I do about her. From the moment I saw her inside the men's bathroom at my club and she gave me her cute little smile and told me thank you, my instinct told me she was different. And after I cornered her at the bar and got a dose of her sassy mouth, and then again at her shop, I knew she was something special. That realization has only grown after spending the last few days with her.

It's not the sex—which is beyond better than anything I've ever experienced. It's just her. She makes me feel like I won the lottery every time I make her laugh. And when I laugh at something she does or says and she gets that pleased look on her face, like I'm giving her a gift, I don't think I have ever seen anything more beautiful. I've never known a woman like her before, and I know I should count myself lucky I stumbled upon her.

When LeFou and I get back up to my condo, I let him off his leash, and he makes a beeline for the bedroom door, nudging it with his nose until he gets in. I enter the room behind him, watching him jump up on the bed, spin around, and then curl up at Chrissie's feet. I change into a pair of sweats before I get into bed and wrap myself around her from behind, and then I bury my face in her hair, breathing her in.

"Gus?" she calls sleepily, threading her fingers between mine against her chest, and I smile at hearing my nickname coming from her for the first time.

"I'm here," I tell her quietly, kissing the back of her head.

"What time is it?" she questions, letting my hand go so she can roll to face me.

"A little after ten."

"Ten," she whispers, sounding horrified as her body grows tight.

I ignore the tightness in her frame and draw her more firmly against me. "How are you feeling?"

"I fell asleep in the car. I . . . you were supposed to go to work," she states, ignoring my question before adding, "I should go home. I'm sure you need to leave."

When she attempts to pull away, I roll her to her back and loom over her. "Work's covered. Now tell me how you're feeling."

"Gaston." She places her hands against my chest.

"How are you feeling?"

"Um. Hungry," she answers, sounding unsure.

I smile, touching my lips to her forehead. "What do you want to eat?"

"Pizza."

"All right." I let her go with one hand, then reach behind me to grab my cell. I pull up the number for the pizza spot down the street, then ask, "What do you want on your pizza?"

"Cheese."

"Just cheese?"

"Yeah."

I press dial, and when someone answers, I place our order, then give them the address and number for my place. They tell me it will be about forty minutes; then I hang up. "We have forty minutes before dinner is here."

"If you have to work, I can—"

"Stop." I cut her off, placing my weight more firmly against her. "I'm here. I want to be here."

"Okay," she breathes as her hands move up my sides, then come to rest against my chest. "I just feel bad that you're here with me instead of focusing on your business."

"Do I look like I'm annoyed that I get the opportunity to spend time with you?"

"Well . . ." She studies my face for a moment before answering. "No."

"That's because I'm not," I tell her, brushing my lips against hers before I lean back. "Now, as I mentioned, we have forty minutes before your pizza gets here, so it's up to you how we spend that time."

"What are my options?" she asks as she glances quickly at my mouth, and I fight back a smile.

"We can either make out"—I touch my lips to hers again, because I can't help myself—"or we can talk about what happened earlier?"

"Make out," she replies instantly, with her voice pitching higher.

I slide my fingers down the side of her face and gentle my tone. "I know that man was your dad and that the woman with him was his wife." Her fingers dig into my flesh as I speak. "You can talk to me, sweetheart."

Her eyes narrow slightly. "Your options weren't really options, were they?"

"What did he say to you?"

"Nothing." She shakes her head.

"Chrissie." I sigh in disappointment.

"No, I mean he didn't say anything. He didn't even notice me when I saw him in the market. His attention was focused on her like she was his whole world. A bomb could have gone off, and neither of them would have noticed." She closes her eyes, but I see the tears she's trying to hide. "He looked happy. All the years growing up with him, I don't remember him ever looking that happy, and I don't know how I never noticed before."

"That caught you off guard, so you ran?" I question, sliding my thumb across her cheek as a single tear slides from underneath her lashes. I capture it on my thumb before she nods, keeping her eyes closed.

"I was . . ." She drags in a shaky breath, then opens her eyes to peer at me. "I had to get away. I couldn't face him. I couldn't face the two of them together."

Seeing the stark pain in her eyes brings the anger I felt earlier back to the surface, and I have the overwhelming urge to hunt down her father and demand answers for his behavior. Having spent years with my mother and my father, I understand better than most that things don't always work out between parents. But no kid, no matter their age, should ever question their parents' love for them.

"You shouldn't have had to be faced with the two of them like that, baby. Your father should have been man enough to contact you and explain things when he decided he was going to leave your mom."

Her expression changes, and I know she's going to defend him. I know, because that's what you do when you love someone: you defend them, even if you know they're in the wrong, and even when you're in pain because of them.

I place my thumb over her lips to keep her quiet and continue. "Even if it would be difficult for him to do, he should have talked to you and your brother and let you each decide how things would eventually play out. He didn't do that. He took the easy way out. He's let you be and continued on with his life."

"It's not like I was a child living at home," she states behind my thumb, and I dip my face closer to hers.

"You're right; you're not a child. You're old enough to understand life, and if he'd given you the opportunity, you could have decided whether or not you'd be comfortable having a relationship with him and the woman he married. You also would have been prepared to see the two of them together, and you wouldn't have been caught off guard."

"I guess you're right," she agrees, sounding annoyed while looking away.

My fingers flex against her cheek, and her eyes come back to mine. "I'm right, sweetheart, and unless he moved to another state, he had to know what happened today was inevitable. Eventually, you'd be in the same place as him and his wife and have to deal with them."

"You're right," she agrees after a few seconds. "I never imagined what would happen when I saw the two of them together. In my head, they were a couple but didn't really exist before I witnessed just how much they mean to each other."

"I think, baby," I start gently, "you need to reconnect with your dad. I know it's not going to be easy, especially after today, but it needs to happen. You live in the same town. I have no doubt you'll see him or her again—honestly, I'm surprised that this is the first time you've seen him. I don't want you to be caught off guard like that again."

"You're right." At her agreement, some of the anxiety leaves my chest, and I'm finally able to relax. She adds, "Maybe I'll call him and see if he's willing to talk to me without her. If he is, I'll see how things go and move forward from there."

"Good, baby, but you should know that no matter what happens, I'll be here to help you sort things out."

Her expression becomes gentle, and then she lifts up to touch her mouth to mine. When she leans back, there's a smile on her face I can't read. I just know in my gut it's good. "Thank you for showing up when you did."

"You're welcome." I roll to my back, bringing her with me, and she plants her hands on my chest and looks down at me curiously. "What?"

"I didn't know you have a motorcycle."

"I have three," I admit while tucking her hair behind her ear.

"Three?" Her eyes widen, making me smile.

"Yeah, besides the one I have here, I've got one in Jersey, at my mom's place, and one in Florida, at her condo."

"Do you ride a lot?"

"All the time—not normally in the winter, but today I knew my bike would get me to you faster than my car," I say.

Her lips part as her eyes fill with tenderness, and then she rests her head against my chest. "Will you take me for a ride sometime?"

"Absolutely, when the weather warms up."

"Awesome." I feel her smile, and I run my fingers through her soft hair as I stare at the ceiling. "Gus?"

"Yeah, babe?"

"I like you a lot."

Fuck. "That's good, sweetheart, because I like you a lot too," I reply, thinking that's a fucking lie, because I'm pretty sure I'm half in love with her already.

Suggestion 9

ADMIT IT TO YOURSELF WHEN YOU FALL FOR HIM

CHRISSIE

"I'll call you as soon as I get home," I tell Gus while trying to ignore the look my best friend is giving me at the moment. One that says she's going to bombard me with questions as soon as I get off the phone.

"Good," he says softly. "I'll bring LeFou down with me. He can stay with you while I'm at work tonight."

"That works for me." A smile I can't help slides into place as happiness and anticipation fill the pit of my stomach. Now, not only do I get to see him tonight, but him bringing LeFou guarantees I will see him again in the morning. "I'll see you when I get home."

"All right, sweetheart. Have fun with your friend."

"I will. Later."

"Later, babe." He hangs up, and I pull my phone from my ear.

"You're in love," Leah shouts, startling me, and I shake my head while she nods. "You are! You're totally in love with this guy."

"I'm not," I deny as my heart suddenly starts to speed up. It's not a lie; I'm not in love with him, but I'm for sure falling hard and fast.

"Your face says you are."

"Leah, I haven't known Gaston long enough to be in love with him. I just . . ." I chew the inside of my cheek, trying to figure out how I feel. "I just like him a lot."

"Looking back, I think I fell in love with Tyler while I was convincing myself we were just friends. You know, that was just a few days after the first time we really spent time together." She and her now husband met under unusual circumstances, and although Leah tried to avoid him, his dog and her cat constantly stirred up trouble, which forced them together.

"Okay, but—"

"Never mind." She cuts me off before I can tell her our circumstances are totally different. "I know I'll never be able to convince you, but I'm just reserving the right to say 'I told you so' when the time comes."

"Whatever." I roll my eyes.

"I have to say . . . ," she starts while flipping open the box on the table between us and inspecting the six cupcakes I brought her. After deciding on a chocolate cupcake with chocolate cherry chip icing and lifting it to her mouth, she says, "It's going to be fun watching you come to terms with things. Now tell me everything about this guy."

"I thought you were feeding me dinner," I prompt as she begins to lick the icing off the top of the cupcake.

"I am." She waves her hand toward her cell. "I called in our order when you let me know you were on your way, so we've got time to talk before our food gets here."

"Can I at least have a glass of wine first?" I ask sarcastically, and she grins.

"Absolutely." She stands, taking her cupcake with her as she walks to the fridge. She pulls out a bottle of my favorite rosé, then pours me a glass and comes back toward the table.

"You're not drinking?" My brows pull together in confusion as she hands me the glass before she takes her seat.

"Well . . ." She looks away, and my eyes narrow.

"Well what?"

"Tyler and I have decided we're going to try to have a baby, and even though I'm not pregnant now, I want to make sure I'm doing everything I can to make that happen for us."

"Oh my God," I whisper, staring at her, and then I set down my glass, stand, and engulf her in a hug. "This is so exciting."

"I'm not pregnant yet." She laughs, and I laugh along with her.

"I don't care; this is awesome." I notice her cheeks have gotten pink, but her eyes have filled with concern. "What?"

"What if it doesn't happen?" she asks softly, sounding worried. We have mutual friends who've tried and never accomplished getting pregnant, so I know her concern is valid.

"It will happen, and when it does, you're going to be an amazing mom," I reassure her.

"I want that." Her expression gentles. "I want to be a mom, but even more, I want Tyler to be a dad."

"It will happen," I repeat. "Just don't stress over it, and have fun trying."

The worry shifts out of her eyes, and happiness takes over her features. "We'll definitely have fun trying."

I laugh as I let her go, then settle into my chair and pick up my glass of wine. "How much fun?"

"You can't even imagine."

"I bet I can." I give her a knowing wink before I take a sip of wine, and she bursts out laughing.

Once she's pulled herself together, she tips her head to the side, studying me before she demands, "Spill."

I smile, take another sip of wine, and then tell her about Gus, starting from the moment he and I met in the men's bathroom. Her eyes are wide as I talk, and they stay that way until our food arrives and she goes to answer the door.

"So he showed up at the grocery store on a motorcycle?" Leah breathes with wide eyes, the forkful of orange chicken and fried rice an inch from her mouth completely forgotten.

"Yeah, pulled right up to my car door, and then he got off and stood there like he was my own personal bodyguard until my dad took his wife's hand and left."

"I think I just fell in love with him," she says, and I smile. "So what happened after that?"

"He dragged me out of my car, put me in the passenger seat, and then drove me home in my car. I fell asleep on the way, then woke up in his bed."

"Holy cow," she whispers.

"I know," I agree quietly, and her eyes fill with concern.

"What are you going to do about your dad?"

"I don't know. Gus says I need to talk to him."

"What do you think?"

"I miss him. I miss having him to lean on. I miss his encouragement and his words of advice."

"I get that," she agrees, reaching for my hand. "He's your dad; you love him."

My chest aches, and I tighten my fingers around hers. "I miss him. I miss who he was to me, but I don't know him anymore. I'm scared, and if I'm honest, I'm really angry with him and I don't know what will happen if I reach out to him. I don't want to be disappointed. He's already turned his back on me once. I don't know if I can handle him doing it again."

"I understand that, but I agree with Gaston. You need to talk to him." Her fingers tighten around mine. "I'm not saying you need to try to patch things up with him, because honestly that's his job, but you need closure. You need to be able to tell your father how you feel, how what he did affected you, and let it go. I know it's not going to be easy, but you'll feel better when it's done."

"You're right." I drag in a breath, and she lets my hand go.

"As for Gaston, or Gus, as you call him—who I want to meet as soon as possible—I can see why you're in love with him."

"You just don't give up, do you?" I laugh, and she grins, giving me a shrug.

Their dog, Bruce, gets up off the kitchen floor, where he's been sprawled out since I got here, and Leah's grin turns into a soft smile. "Tyler's home," she tells me, and then I hear the front door open and Tyler's voice float into the kitchen from the living room.

"Babe?"

"In the kitchen with Chrissie," she calls back, and two seconds later, he appears in the doorway. "How was work?"

"Work," he responds, coming across the room. Once he's close, he threads his fingers through her hair at the back of her head and bends to touch his mouth to hers. My stomach flips, so I have no doubt Leah's does the same. When he pulls back, he smiles at her, then turns to look at me. "Hey, Chrissie."

"Hey." I laugh, and he grins. Seriously, my best friend might've had some really bad relationships, but she struck a home run when she met Tyler. They couldn't be more perfect for each other. "How was the honeymoon?" I ask as he opens the box of cupcakes.

"Over too quickly."

"I agree," Leah says, looking up at her husband. "I ordered you beef and broccoli. It's in the bag on the counter."

"Thanks, baby. Gonna shower, then I'll come eat." At the mention of a shower, I see Leah's eyes dilate, and I know that's my cue to leave.

"I'm going to take off," I say, and they both look at me like they forgot I was even in the room.

"You don't have to go," Tyler tells me, and I grin.

"Sorry, big guy. I think I do." I stand, closing up my food I will take with me and eat later. "Oh, before I forget." I look between the two of them. "My brother and his partner are coming in for New Year's, so

I'm having a small get-together at my place to watch the fireworks, if you want to join us."

"Is Gus going to be there?" Leah questions.

Tyler looks down at her and asks, "Gus?"

"Gaston, Chrissie's boyfriend."

"Right." He nods.

"I'm not sure," I answer with a shrug. "I haven't asked him yet, and I don't know if he'll be able to because of work. It's just a guess, but I imagine New Year's is a busy night for him."

"True," Leah agrees. Then she adds, "We don't have plans, so we'll be there."

"Awesome. Chris will be excited to see you." I put on my jacket and grab my purse. "Now, give me a hug so I can get out of here and you two can go shower."

Leah laughs, giving me a hug, and Tyler chuckles. After I get a hug from him, Leah walks me to the front door, then waves goodbye from the porch as I get into my car. I blow her a kiss and she catches it, and then with a smile on her face, she heads back inside. I drive home and call Gus on the way to let him know I'll be there soon, and when I arrive about twenty minutes later, I park and go into the lobby. As soon as I clear the door, my eyes meet Gaston's, and he smiles while LeFou tugs at his leash to get to me. My stomach fills with a strange sense of contentment.

"You couldn't wait to see me?" I tease while I pick up LeFou and kiss the top of his head.

"No," Gaston answers, making my heart skip a beat. "I missed you all damn day."

"I missed you too." I tip my head back to accept his kiss when he bends to touch his mouth to mine. "Did you get things sorted with the order?" I ask.

"No. The truck driver insists he did a count when he dropped off the order. He's adamant it was all there and that a woman accepted the order and signed off on it. That could only have been my bar manager, Georgia, but she says she never signed for the order; she just found it next to the back door, did a count, and knew it was off, so she called me."

"Did you check the signature?"

"I checked. It wasn't Georgia's, and she was the only woman there yesterday afternoon."

My brows pull together. "Do you have cameras?"

"I do, but the one at the back door went out about a week ago, and the guy who set them up is out of town until next week."

"That's odd, isn't it?" The whole situation just seems weird.

"Not really. The cameras go out from time to time. It just sucks that this happened when that one was down."

"I'm sorry, honey."

His eyes soften and he bends, touching his lips to mine again then pulling back. "I'll get it sorted." He takes LeFou from me and places him on the ground, then takes my hand and leads me toward the elevator. Once we're inside, he presses the button for his floor, and I raise a brow in question. "I'm gonna change for work, then grab LeFou's dishes and some of his food so I won't have to do it in the morning when I get home."

"Bummer."

"What?" he asks, dipping his head toward me.

"I thought maybe you were taking me to your place to have your way with me on your giant, comfortable bed," I say, watching his eyes grow dark as I speak. "I'm just bummed that's not what's happening."

"Oh, that's definitely happening," he rumbles, pressing me back against the wall of the elevator, with one hand going to my hip and the other wrapping around the back of my skull. I feel his fingers lace through my hair; I pull back and give him full control over me as he lowers his head and proceeds to devour my mouth.

We make out until the doors slide open, and I'm lightheaded and drunk on his kiss as he takes my hand and pulls me down the hall. I giggle at his hurried pace, and he grunts at me, making me laugh harder as he unlocks the door. After letting LeFou off his leash, he takes my purse from me, putting it on the counter in the kitchen, and then turns in my direction, his dark eyes filled with mischief.

"Why are you looking at me like that?" I question, taking a step back, and he grins playfully right before he lunges, catches me around the waist, and lifts me off the ground. I squeal as he tosses me over his shoulder, and then I laugh, holding on as he runs with me bouncing like a sack of potatoes.

Before I can prepare, I'm flying through the air, then landing with a bounce on his bed. I giggle as he lands on me and grins. "You're not going to be laughing in a second, sweetheart."

"We'll see." I smirk.

"Challenge accepted," he rasps out, right before he has his way with me in his giant bed, giving me two really great orgasms before finding his own release.

On my belly with the blanket up over my hips, I open one eye when I feel his hand against my lower back and see his pompous smile. "Don't be annoying," I mutter, and he chuckles.

"Wanna shower with me?"

"No, I can't move, and your bed is seriously comfortable," I say. His expression turns smug, and I narrow my eyes. "Whatever, go shower." I hear him laugh as I close my eyes, but I honestly don't care.

I fall into an exhausted sleep, then come awake to him softly kissing my brow.

"Why don't you just stay here?" he suggests, leaning back to catch my eye.

"I want to take a bath," I tell him. For the last few nights, I haven't had a chance to enjoy my nightly ritual, and I miss it.

"I have one of those." He smiles while gliding his fingers down the side of my face.

"I know," I say, feeling a little jealous. His bath, which he probably never uses, is way bigger than mine, with a dozen jets that look like they would be amazing when active.

"All right, so take a bath here."

"I don't have my bath stuff."

"I'll give you my key. You can go down to your place, pack a bag, and then come back here, take a bath, snoop through all my stuff, and then sleep in my bed."

"I wouldn't snoop through your stuff," I huff.

"Why not?"

"Because that's rude."

"Babe, if you left me alone in your place, I'd for sure snoop through your stuff."

"Liar." I shake my head while smiling.

"Sleep here," he orders, looming over me.

"You won't mind?"

"Coming home to find you in my bed? No, sweetheart, I definitely won't mind that."

Seriously, I'm starting to think Leah was right about me being in love with this man.

"All right, I'll stay."

"Good." He smiles as he places his lips against mine, then pulls back and stands. "I'll leave the key on the counter in the kitchen for you."

"Should I take LeFou out?" I ask, and hearing his name, LeFou jumps up onto the bed and begins attacking me with doggie kisses, making me laugh. I sit up, cuddling him close to my chest in an attempt to control his wiggling body.

"He should be good. If he's not, he'll let you know, and you can let him out onto the patio. There's a patch of grass in a box that he uses at night sometimes."

"His own patch of grass twenty-plus stories in the air? How fancy." I grin, and as he laughs, I take a moment to appreciate the sound, along with the way he looks wearing dark-gray slacks and an emerald-green shirt that does amazing things to his eyes.

"You need to stop looking at me like that, sweetheart. Otherwise, I'm not going to be able to leave."

"Give me a second. I'm almost done," I tell him.

He shakes his head, smiling, then steps toward the bed, taking hold of my jaw before he bends to kiss me deeply. When he pulls an inch away, my eyes flutter open. "Be good, and I'll see you in the morning."

"You will," I agree breathlessly, right before he touches his mouth to mine one last time and stands to his full height.

I watch him leave the room and listen for the sound of the front door closing behind him while I continue to cuddle LeFou in my lap. I eventually get up and put on my clothes, and once I'm dressed, I go to the kitchen and then grab the key he left for me and my keys from my purse. I head to my place, gathering everything I'll need for my bath. I also pack a nightgown and the stuff I'll need in the morning to get ready for work in one of my overnight bags. I check the bag before zipping it up to make sure I'm not forgetting anything, then carry it upstairs.

As soon as I let myself into Gus's place, LeFou greets me at the door, then follows me into the kitchen, where I leave both sets of keys on the counter. I shut him in with me in the bathroom, then start the bath, and as I wait for the giant tub to fill, I strip out of my clothes and put on my robe before I give myself a facial. With my face mask on, I leave the bathroom and go to the kitchen to pour a glass of wine and put the Chinese food I forgot about in the fridge. I grab my phone and find a text from Gaston.

At work, but wishing I was with you.

I can't help the girly sigh that leaves my mouth or the butterflies that fill my stomach as I read his message again.

I bite my lip as I type back.

I'm getting in the bath. Wish you were here to join me.

Not even five seconds after I press send does he message back with all caps.

THIS NIGHT IS GOING TO FUCKING DRAG.

I laugh as I message back, Sorry ☹

I take my phone and wine with me to the bathroom, and my little furry shadow follows close at my heels. Thankfully, the tub is half-full, so I dump in a few scoops of my bath salts and climb in. I instantly relax in the hot water and sip from my glass, with LeFou standing at the side of the tub on his hind legs, woofing quietly while studying me with doggie concern.

"I'm just taking a bath," I reassure him as I pet the top of his head. Eventually, he decides I'm okay and he can get down to doing more important things, like taking a nap. As I soak, he curls into a ball on the deep-blue, fluffy rug that runs the length of the vanity, but as soon as the tub is full enough for me to turn on the jets, I do, and he wakes up.

He comes back to investigate the noise and the water as it swirls around me, and a couple of times I actually think he might jump high enough to throw himself over the lip of the tub and in with me. That doesn't happen, but while the jets are going, he stays at the edge looking in excitedly.

After my body feels like a limp noodle, I get out and towel off. I want to get into bed, but my stomach growling as I put on my nightgown forces me to leave the room and go to the kitchen, taking my empty glass with me, along with LeFou. I dump my leftover Chinese food into a bowl and heat it up, then make myself comfortable on the couch and eat while I watch a crime show on TV that I probably shouldn't watch when alone in a place that's not my own in the dark of night.

After I've finished eating and am completely freaked out, I let LeFou out onto the patio when he goes to the door, hitting it with his tiny paw and demanding out. I wait for him to come back in, then carry him with me to the bedroom, shutting the door and then locking it for good measure. I leave the bedside lamp on after I get into bed, and LeFou forces his way under the covers, then settles in against my stomach. I pet the top of his furry head as I look around and notice that, besides the expensive furniture, the room is bare. There isn't even a single piece of art hanging on the gray walls.

Hearing a noise, I jump, and my heart starts to race. "It's probably just a neighbor," I tell myself, but I jump again when there's a squeak. Feeling overwhelmingly out of place, I flip back the blankets, making LeFou jump. "Sorry, boy. I can't sleep here. We're going down to my place," I tell him before I get out of the bed.

He jumps down and circles my feet as I go to the dresser. I find a pair of flannel sleep pants, along with a long-sleeved cotton T-shirt, and put both items on over my nightgown. Once I'm covered, I grab my cell phone and pick up LeFou. I open the door and peek out just in case someone has snuck in to murder me. When I see the coast is clear, I hurry to the kitchen to get my keys, then run to the front door like someone is chasing me.

When I make it into the brightly lit hall, I let out the breath I've been holding and go to the elevator. Once I'm locked in safe and secure in my space, I get into bed and send Gaston a text letting him know where he will find me and LeFou in the morning. My cell phone rings a moment later, making me jump, and I roll my eyes at my craziness, then slide my finger across the screen and put my cell to my ear. "Hey."

"Are you okay?" he asks as I lean back against my pillows while LeFou explores my room.

"Yeah. I just freaked myself out and wanted to be in my space."

"How'd you freak yourself out?" he questions, and I notice I don't hear the sound of music in the background, which makes me curious about where he is right now.

"I somehow ended up watching a crime show, and obviously that wasn't a good idea."

"I see." There's no mistaking the smile I hear in his voice.

"So, I'm fine. I'm just a dork."

"An adorable dork."

"Glad you think so," I say, wondering if I've ever been this happy before. "It's really quiet. Are you still at the club?"

"Yeah, I stepped into my office when I got your text. Now I'm sitting at my desk, wondering how pissed Luke would be if I called him in to cover for me."

He told me about his best friend, Luke, last night after I asked who was taking care of his business while he was taking care of me. I was surprised to find out Luke already knew about me, since in most of my previous relationships that didn't happen until things were kind of serious.

"Probably pretty pissed, if he's home with his family," I say quietly.

"You're probably right." He sighs, sounding aggravated. I know I shouldn't like that he is frustrated right now, but I still really like that he wants to be here with me. "You sure you're okay?"

"I'm sure. Now that I'm in my space, I'm good, and after LeFou finishes sniffing around and comes to cuddle with me, I'm going to go to sleep."

"Now I'm jealous of my dog," he grumbles, making me laugh. "Glad you're finding this funny."

"It's a little funny," I tell him through my laughter.

"You're not the one sitting here wishing away time, baby," he says softly, and then his voice changes as he calls, "Come in," so I know he's not talking to me.

I hear a woman's sultry voice say Gaston's name, but I can't make out what she's saying with the music that is now playing in the background. "I'll be there to help you in a second, Georgia," Gus tells her, and a second later the music dies. "Sorry, baby. I gotta go. I'll see you in the morning." I want to ask what he's helping sexy-voice Georgia with, but before I can open my mouth, the phone goes dead. I pull it from my ear and stare at it for a second, then drop it to my side table.

"Come on, LeFou. Time to explore is over," I say in his direction, pulling his attention away from the pile of clothes in the corner of the room he's sniffing at. His fluffy white head turns, and I pat the bed. "Come on. It's time to sleep." He runs toward me, then jumps up onto the bed and licks my face. "Sleep." I rub the top of his head with one hand, then reach over to turn out the lamp. Once the room is plunged into darkness, he burrows under the covers, settles in against my stomach, and falls asleep. And after an hour of replaying the sound of Georgia saying Gaston's name and reminding myself that he's never given me a reason to be jealous, I thankfully am able to fall asleep.

Suggestion 10

DON'T BE AFRAID TO ADD A LITTLE COLOR TO

HIS LIFE

CHRISSIE

Completely sated and sprawled out half on top of Gaston, I listen to his heartbeat while my fingers scribble random patterns along his rib cage. It's been two weeks since the night I attempted to stay at his place, and since then, we've fallen into a routine. When I get home from work, he brings LeFou to me, and we have dinner or just spend a few hours together before he has to leave. And when he gets home in the morning, we spend a couple more hours, usually in bed, before I have to get up. It never feels like enough time, but I still enjoy every second of it.

"What's your plan for Christmas Day?" I ask Gaston as I lazily lift my cheek off his bare chest to look at him.

"I'll spend the morning at home, then go to Luke's around three or four for dinner. What about you? Are you still planning on going to your mom's?"

"Yeah, I'll go over in the afternoon. She told me she's already got most of the groceries and that she wants to cook for me this year, so I won't have to be there so early."

"That's good news, baby."

"Yeah." It is good. My mom has seemed more like herself the last few times we've spoken, and her making an effort with Christmas is a huge step, especially after the way last year ended.

"How about you stay with me Christmas Eve, and we spend Christmas morning together?" he asks, and I melt into him.

"How about you stay with me, since you don't have a tree, and I'll make you my cream cheese–stuffed french toast?"

"Sounds good." He smiles while running his finger along the edge of my hairline. "My mom's coming in for New Year's, and I'd like you to meet her while she's here."

My heart starts to beat a little faster. Making plans to see each other on Christmas and him wanting me to meet his mom tell me he's in just as deep as I am. He's so different from all the other men I've dated. He's honest, which makes me feel secure; I never have to question what he means when he says or does something, because he tells it like it is. If he were any other guy, I'd be questioning how quickly things are progressing between us, but with him this just feels right.

"I'd like that," I say, and he looks pleased with my response. "My brother and his boyfriend are flying in to ring in the New Year with me, so I'm having a small gathering at my place. There's not going to be a lot of people, but my best friend and her husband are coming. I'll have food and drinks. I'd love you to be there, and your mom is welcome to come."

"I work that night, but maybe we can split things up. You can come to the club, hang in VIP with your people for a few hours, and then I'll come back with you, and we can ring in the New Year before I go back to work."

"I like that idea. Let me just talk to Leah and my brother and see what they say."

"Is your mom going to be here for New Year's Eve?"

"I'm not sure. I mentioned it to her, but she didn't say yes or no."

"I'd like to meet her sometime," he says, and my stomach drops.

I still haven't told my mom about him. I guess I wanted to be sure she was actually moving on with her life before I told her about Gus. I didn't want her negativity tainting what we're building, but I do plan—if all goes well on Christmas—to tell her about him then.

"I'm guessing from the look on your face she doesn't know about me," he says casually, and he doesn't look mad, just reflective.

"It's really creepy that you can read me so easily."

"Talk to me," he orders, leaving no room for argument.

"Fine," I sigh. "The night she called me freaking out about my dad taking his wife to Hawaii, she made me promise to never trust a man the way she trusted my dad."

"That explains you going from hot to cold that night," he mumbles while absently playing with a lock of my hair.

"I want to tell her about us," I say quietly. "I just want to make sure she is really in a good place before I do."

"I get that, baby."

"You do?" I ask.

"I'm not saying I'll be happy if you don't ever tell your mom about us, but I understand why you haven't yet. When the time is right, you'll know, and when that happens, I'd like to meet her."

"Are you an alien?" I blurt, studying him in disbelief.

His brows snap together, and he asks, "What?"

"You can't possibly be from Earth. First, you're too hot." I hold up one finger. "Second, your skills in the bedroom are out of this world." I hold up another finger, and his lips twitch. "And third, you're too understanding." I shake my head. "The only explanation is you're not actually from here, but from some far-off galaxy, and your spaceship crash-landed, leaving you stranded on this planet for the rest of your life."

"As much as I enjoy you pointing out that you think I'm hot, amazing in bed, and smart enough to know what battles to pick," he says, with humor lacing his tone, "I'm sorry to disappoint you, babe. I'm just your everyday earthling."

"You probably wouldn't tell me if you were an alien. It would be unfortunate if the government found out about your existence, kidnapped you, and started experimenting."

His head falls back to the pillow as he laughs; then he mutters, "Yeah, that would be unfortunate."

"Especially the probing. The probing would probably really suck."

I start to laugh as he growls, sitting up with his arms wrapped around me, but I stop laughing and start breathing deeply when he rolls me to my back and settles himself between my thighs. "I think we should test out this probing you're talking about."

"I think that would be smart," I agree breathlessly as the head of his cock nudges my entrance.

His eyes lock on mine as he slides slowly inside me, and I tighten around him every way I can. My fingers dig into his ribs, my legs lift to wrap around his hips, and the walls of my sex contract. I watch the muscles in his strong jaw twitch as he fills me completely, and I relish the slight sting of beautiful pain that always comes when he is deep within me. I soak up the look in his eyes as they bore into mine, then moan as he slowly pulls back his hips.

"Never, not fucking ever, have I felt anything as beautiful as your pussy surrounding me, holding tight, locking me deep," he groans.

I whimper my agreement, then lift my head as he drops his lower to kiss me. My mouth opens, and when his tongue touches mine, I lose myself in him completely. Like every time we've made love, the world outside our connection ceases to exist. It's just him and me, the two of us connecting body and soul.

He rocks into me slowly, and I accept each and every thrust, building higher and higher until I'm close to the edge of euphoria. I call out his name as my body takes over, and he falls with me, holding me, kissing me, giving me everything while sending me flying. I've never had what I have with him, and I know without a shadow of a doubt that I'll never have this with anyone else.

When he pulls his mouth from mine and drops it to my shoulder to kiss me, tears start to sting behind my eyes, but I fight the urge to cry, not wanting to ruin whatever just happened between us with too many emotions. He rolls us until I'm once more draped across his chest; then his fingers slowly slide through my hair and down my spine.

"Didn't use a condom." His words swiftly pull me from my happy, relaxed state, and I lift my head to look at him. "You're safe with me in all the ways you can be, sweetheart, but I wanted you to know I didn't use a condom."

"I'm on birth control."

"I know." He smiles an odd smile. "I spotted your pills when I was snooping through your shit." His joke instantly lightens the intensity of the moment, and I relax.

"What else have you found while snooping through my stuff?"

"Sadly, nothing. I think I need some time alone in your space to do a better job."

"Tomorrow while I'm at work, you can take your time. Just don't open my nightstand."

"Why's that?"

"Because in there, you'll be forced to meet Bob without me, and I'd rather be around for that introduction."

"Bob?" He raises one brow.

"Bob is my battery-operated boyfriend. We hook up from time to time."

"Oh." His eyes light up. "I think you, me, and Bob are going to be great friends."

"We'll see." I smile, then kiss the middle of his chest, ignoring the twist of desire in my lower belly. "How much more time do I have with you before you have to leave to go to work?" I ask, and he leans his head back to look at the alarm clock on my bedside table, then grumbles something I can't make out. "I'm going to guess not long."

"Sorry, baby." He looks at me. "Shit's been crazy. We've been short employees at the club and both bars with everyone traveling for the holidays. Last night, I ended up bartending, and I was so desperate I had to force Luke behind the bar for a couple hours, which he was not happy about. He's not a people person, and women who are not his wife annoy him, so that went about as well as it could go."

"How many times a night do you get hit on?" I ask out of curiosity and then answer for him when he doesn't. "I bet it's a lot. I'd totally flirt with you."

"Baby, you met me in my club and told me straight out that I should leave you alone."

My nose scrunches. "Oh yeah, I forgot about that," I mumble, and he starts to laugh. "Anyway." I get back on point. "I can come help out," I say, leaning away, but I don't get far. His hands wrap around my hips to keep me in place, and I smile before I continue. "I haven't ever bartended, but I've done a lot of waitressing."

"You'd do that, wouldn't you? Work all damn day at your shop, then step in to help me out and work some more."

"I'm not saying I'd stay all night."

"You'd do that, though, if I needed it."

He's right; I would do that.

He sits up while wrapping his hand around the nape of my neck; then his lips touch my forehead. "As much as I'd love getting some more time with you, you work enough already. You need to rest. That said, I really appreciate you offering to help me out. It means a lot."

"Well, if you change your mind, you know where to find me."

"Yeah." He rolls me to my back, kisses me swiftly, and then pushes off me and the bed. I watch with fascination while his muscles flex as he walks naked around the room, and then I rest my head on my pillow. "Has Josh gotten back to you with any news about your books?"

"Not yet. I imagine I should hear from him before Christmas, but if I don't, I'll call him after the holiday."

"It would be good if you had some help, baby. I know the girls being on Christmas break right now is helping you out, especially with how busy you are with everyone placing orders for the holidays. But they gotta go back to school after New Year's, and when that happens, you're going to be on your own again. I don't like that much, because I know your workload is only going to increase. Plus, I'd like to be able to have one if not a couple days a week with you. Days we could spend in bed, or out on my bike when the weather warms up."

"I'll call Josh today and see if he's got any news," I say as my mind spins with everything he's just said. It's so odd to have a man who actually pays attention to what I say and supports me and my career. "I'd like to have lazy days with you and am really looking forward to riding on your bike."

"Me too, baby." He gives me a smile; then his eyes roam my face and chest. "I also need to figure some shit out, because I really fucking don't like leaving you in bed every night while I go to work."

"It's okay," I reassure him, sitting up and pulling the blanket up and tucking it under my arms.

"Right now it's okay, but eventually it won't be, and I can't expect you to make changes to make me happy and for me not to do the same in return."

"I'm happy." I frown.

"Yeah, I know that, but you don't think it's gonna get old, me leaving late at night and you sleeping alone? Or let's say this keeps building between us, and we get to the point where we have a kid together. Do you think you'd be cool with me being out all night, leaving you at home with a baby, and then sleeping all day, leaving you to parent on your own?" He wraps his hands around his hips.

With my heart pounding hard, my mouth dry, and my stomach dropping to my toes, I shake my head, wondering how I went from never thinking I'd find someone to having a conversation with a man about having kids one day. "No . . . no, I don't think I'd like that much."

"Exactly, and I'm not saying I'll hire another manager to run the bars at night right now, but I will see if Luke can change up his schedule a little so a couple nights a week I can be here with you."

"I'd like it if you did that." My tone is still quiet.

His hands drop from his hips; then his head tips to the side. "You wanna shower with me?" For once, I'm not asleep or half-asleep, so I nod. "Then hurry, baby, or I'm going to be late."

"You do know you could have just gotten in the shower without me, right?"

"Why on earth would I do that?"

"Because you're obviously in a hurry." I roll my eyes as I get out of bed.

"Just move your cute ass." He slaps my bottom as I walk past him, making me jump.

I turn my head to narrow my eyes on him over my shoulder, but his eyes aren't on mine. They're glued to the area where his hand just landed. "Eyes up here, buddy," I call, and he smirks.

I ignore his look and walk into the bathroom, flipping on the lights, and then go to the shower and turn it on. While the water warms up, we stand side by side brushing our teeth, and when we're done, we get into the shower together. He places me under the warm water first, tipping my head back to soak my hair, then surprises me by asking for my shampoo. I hand him the bottle, and he squeezes way more than I ever use into his big hand before he thoroughly massages it in with his fingers, rinsing away the suds before asking for my conditioner.

I hand it over and watch as he repeats the same actions as before, and when he's finished, he moves me out from under the spray and grabs one of my three loofas, a bright-yellow one that has roughened edges to help with exfoliating. I pick up my pink one and dump some of my vanilla bodywash on it, rubbing it into the material and causing it to bubble up while he examines the built-in shelf where all my body-washes are lined up.

"If you're trying to figure out which one won't leave you smelling like cake or flowers, this one will have to do." I hand him one that smells like peppermint, and he takes it from me, clicking open the lid, then sniffing.

"I need to leave some of my shit down here," he mutters, making me smile. He squeezes the peppermint wash on his loofa, then scrubs it against his chest before moving it over every perfect inch of his body.

I forget I'm actually supposed to be washing myself as I watch the sudsy water slide down his smooth skin, getting caught here and there between the contours and ridges of his muscles. "Do you work out?" I ask him, slightly dazed as I look up to meet his gaze.

"Yeah, most days I run, and a few days a week I go to the gym," he answers absently as he places the loofa on its hook. I've never seen him work out, so he must do it when I'm at work.

"It shows. You have a great body."

He drags the piece of material out of my hands, and I look down, noticing I've created a lake of bubbles at my feet. "In case you're wondering, I love your body too, so whatever it is you're doing, keep that up."

I can't help the smile that twitches my lips any more than I can control the slight whimper that escapes as he washes me from my neck down to my toes. When he's finished with his task and I'm thoroughly clean, he turns me under the water and rinses me off before pulling down on the handle, bringing our shower to an end.

He opens the glass door and steps out, grabbing one of my fluffy dark-pink towels and wrapping it around his hips before nabbing another and shaking it out. He holds it open to me, and I step forward as he swings it around my back, then wraps me up like one would a small child.

"Thanks."

He smiles, then kisses my forehead, releasing me to take a step back, remove his towel from his waist, and dry off. I don't watch, because I know if I do I'll end up going to bed without my hair brushed or my night cream on my face.

"I'll take LeFou out one last time before I go to work," he tells me as I begin to pull my brush through my wet hair, and I meet his gaze in the mirror.

"I don't mind taking him out."

He shakes his head in denial. "I'll take him before I go. I'll also order another one of his potty boxes for your patio, so if he's here with you, you don't feel like you have to get dressed to take him out at night. Instead, you can just let him out when he needs to go."

"Bodywash in my shower and a potty box on my patio. I'm starting to think you're going to be here a lot."

"Only until I can get you used to being in my home alone without running away in the middle of the night."

"Your place doesn't look like a home. It looks like a showplace. Besides the few photos in your living room giving that space some character, I'd never know someone actually lived there. You don't even have any art on the walls, and the things you do own are all varying shades of gray and black. The night I 'ran away,' as you put it, I felt like I was in a cell and it was closing in around me." He looks away from me to glance around my bathroom.

I know what he sees without looking—gold wallpaper with a very cool design, vibrant floral face towels hanging above each sink, and two pieces of floral art hanging on the wall. My entire place is decorated much the same, with lots of bright colors here and there bringing life to my space. Since I can remember, I've surrounded myself with lots of color, and the way I decorated after I bought my condo is no different. Even the utensils most people never see that are tucked away in the drawers of my kitchen are bright and colorful. I could never live a life surrounded by black and white. I'd probably go crazy if I tried.

"If we need to add some color to my place in order for you to stay there, then we'll do that," he says, and I swear my mouth drops open. He studies my face for a moment, then adds, "Just no flowers."

"You don't like flowers?" I question with a straight face, even though I really, really want to laugh.

"Babe," is all he says.

I start to giggle, and he shakes his head before disappearing into my room. After I finish brushing my hair, I tie it up into a ponytail, then apply my night cream and leave the bathroom. I find Gaston without a shirt but with his slacks on, sitting on the side of my bed and putting on his shoes. I walk to my dresser, open my top drawer, and grab the first nightgown my hand lands on.

I remove my towel, tossing it to the end of the bed before pulling the nightgown on over my head. When I feel eyes on me, I look at Gaston, who's still bent with his fingers around the laces of his shoes but his eyes on me. I ignore his heated gaze, walk across the room, and open the door as I call out to LeFou. I listen to his tags jingle and his nails clicking against the hardwood as he runs full speed from wherever he's been hanging out since he was locked out an hour ago.

A tiny white blur zooms by me, and since he's going fast, he can't stop. He slides across the wood floor, only halting when he hits the carpet and tumbles, making me gasp with worry. Obviously no worse for wear, he quickly finds his feet and bounces excitedly toward me.

"Don't scare me like that," I scold him before scooping him up and holding his wiggling body firmly against my chest. He licks my chin in apology, and I kiss the top of his head as I get into bed. I sit Indian-style with my back to my headboard, then drag my paisley-printed duvet over my lap and settle him on top of the covers. I rub the top of his head as I watch unapologetically as Gaston stands, picks up his shirt, and shrugs it on, hiding his amazing body one button at a time. When the show is over, I let out a sigh of happiness, then tip my head back when he steps toward the bed, grinning.

"I'll be back in a few." He bends to kiss me while simultaneously extracting LeFou from my hold, and I nod.

I watch the two of them leave my room, then find the remote for my TV in my bedside table. I flip on the television, then lift the remote to my lips. "Hallmark Channel," I say, and like magic, the channel changes. While I wait for my guys to come back, I lie back in bed and start to watch two people as they begin to fall unexpectedly in love during the Christmas holiday.

Gaston reappears with LeFou during a commercial a while later, and I get out of bed to walk him to the front door. As usual, our goodbye includes a long make-out session, so by the time I crawl back into bed, the couple on TV is working through some drama. I shut off the television after I know they'll be okay and fall asleep with LeFou resting on my feet, and I wish I was going to bed with Gaston holding me.

Suggestion 11

BE VERY CLEAR

GASTON

I walk into my office and close the door behind me, blocking out the heavy music coming from the club just feet away. I soak up the silence while I slip off my suit jacket and hang it up. I grab my cell from the pocket of my slacks to call Chrissie for no other reason than to hear her voice, but I stop when a knock sounds on the door a second later as I'm taking a seat behind my desk.

I bite back a groan of annoyance. With just days until Christmas, and New Year's coming up quickly, things have been crazier than usual, which isn't unexpected, since New Year's Eve is one of my busiest nights. Every spare second I've had has been filled with talking to my liquor distributors, making sure we have enough staff on at the club along with both bars, and hiring extra security for all three locations for the night. I scrub my hands down my face, wishing I was at home with my woman in bed and watching one of her TV shows.

"Come in!" I shout.

"Sorry, Gus." Georgia peeks her blonde head in. "Do you have a minute?"

"Yeah." I lean back in my chair and watch her shut the door and strut toward me in jeans that are so tight they look painted on and the club's uniform black T-shirt with TWILIGHT written across the front in bold, shimmering letters. A shirt she's altered, cutting away the neck so it hangs off one shoulder, and most of the bottom, so you can see a whole lot of skin between the shirt and the top of her jeans. I'm not surprised by the amount of skin she's showing, nor do I care. Most of the girls have destroyed their shirts with scissors to help maximize tips, and in my opinion, they can have at it as long as they don't fuck around on the job and they keep the paying customers happy.

"What's up?" I question and then frown as she walks around the corner of my desk and plants herself on the edge facing me. She's so close her leg brushes mine. I move away, but not to be deterred, she leans toward me in a blatant attempt to show off her cleavage, along with her lace bra.

"I wanted to go over the plans for the VIP sections on New Year's with you."

"Can you do that sitting somewhere else?" I ask, and she shrugs one shoulder with what I'm sure she thinks is a coy smile playing on her lips. "It wasn't a question. It was a request, Georgia," I state firmly, making my point clear by indicating one of the two chairs across from me.

"Sorry." She at least has the good sense to look somewhat embarrassed.

I'm not stupid. I know she has a crush on me. If her subtle flirting didn't clue me in, her not-so-subtle advances—which I've continuously blocked—would have. She's pretty enough, but I have never been interested in her, and not just because it would be stupid to go there with an employee. She's straight up not my type. She's too skinny, too forward, and too money hungry for my taste. I've made it clear on more than one occasion that nothing is ever going to happen between us, but she's the type of woman who normally hooks any guy she wants, so she's convinced herself I'm playing a game I'm not actually playing.

"What about VIP?" I ask once she's seated in the chair in front of my desk.

"I saw you blocked off one of the sections for your personal guests on New Year's. I know you mentioned your mom coming into town, so if it's only her, I thought we could do a little rearranging so we're not missing out on paying customers. I'll have the guys help me set up a special table just for her on the VIP platform, and—"

"Leave it like it is," I say, cutting her off.

"Gus." She says my name with a placating smile, like she's talking to an unruly child. "The VIP section on New Year's is big money for the club, and in turn big tips for the waitstaff. I don't know if blocking off one huge area for your mom is smart."

My already-frayed temper begins to unravel, and I count to ten in my head so I don't lose my shit. It doesn't help.

"First, I've owned this club for almost five years. You might manage the bar here, but this is *my* club, so do not ever question me." Her eyes are wide as she starts to open her mouth, but I continue on before she can speak. "I appreciate you looking out for my bottom line and your girls, but it's not necessary. My mother, my girlfriend, her brother, and a few other people will be taking the section I blocked off. They won't be staying until midnight, so when they decide to leave—which will probably be early—we will place another group of people in that section." I know they'll be leaving early, since Chrissie called her brother and Leah yesterday afternoon. She checked to see if they would want to join her at the club before going back to her place to watch the fireworks, and they all agreed they would.

"Girlfriend?" she whispers, like it's the only word she actually heard, making my jaw clench tight. "I didn't know you have a girlfriend."

Her hurt-filled tone pisses me off, and I know it's time to take Luke's advice and settle this shit once and for all. I lean forward in my chair, placing my hands on the top of my desk. "Yes, I have a girlfriend, and like I've told you before, Georgia, nothing is ever going to happen between you and me."

"That wasn't—"

"Don't." I hold up my hand, cutting her off, knowing she's going to try to save face, because she's embarrassed that I called her out. "If you can't handle running my bar, being professional, and doing your job, tell me now. You can quit, or put in your two weeks' notice, finish out your time, and find somewhere else to work."

Her face pales, and her expression turns to one of stunned disbelief and pain, and I want to kick my own ass for not dealing with this situation sooner. Luke told me a long time ago that I needed to set her straight, but I figured if I didn't give her any indication that I was even the slightest bit interested, she'd get over her crush and move on. Apparently, I was wrong.

"What's it gonna be, Georgia? Because honest to God, we're not having this conversation ever fuckin' again."

"I . . ." She swallows, looking over my shoulder and stating softly, "I like working here."

"That's good, because you're an asset to this club," I tell her truthfully. "Every employee respects you, you're always here when you're supposed to be, and besides Luke, you're one of the few people I trust." At my statement, her hopeful gaze comes back to me. "That being the case, I need to know you've heard what I've said."

"I can be professional," she agrees, and I lift my chin in approval before she lowers her eyes to the top of my desk.

"Is there anything else we need to discuss right now?"

"No." She shakes her head as she gets up.

"All right. I've got some stuff to take care of here. Then I'll come out to let you all know when I'm leaving to go check on the bars."

"Okay." She averts her eyes as she walks out of my office and closes the door.

"Fuck." I pull my fingers through my hair, then grab my cell phone out of my pocket.

I dial Chrissie and listen as the phone rings. When her soft, sweet voice greets me with a sleepy "Hey," my body relaxes. I talk to her for a good half hour while I go through my emails, and then I tell her I'll see her in the morning when she starts to sound like she's falling back to sleep.

After I get off the phone with her, I walk through the club, letting everyone who needs to know that I'm leaving. I spend the rest of the night between my two bars, and at the end of the night, I do drawer counts at all three of my businesses, then do a bank run. I make a deposit of all the cash that's come in so I don't have to keep it in the safe at the club. Exhausted after a long night, I head home, looking forward to the few hours I get to spend with my woman before she has to leave for work later in the morning.

An hour later, I use the key Chrissie gave me to let myself into her place, and LeFou greets me at the door, then follows me to her dark bedroom and into the bathroom. I strip out of my clothes, brush my teeth, and then shut off the light before I open the door so I don't wake her, since she has a couple of hours before she actually has to get up. As soon as I slide under the blankets, she turns toward me, whispering, "Gus."

I curl her into my side and whisper, "Go back to sleep, sweetheart," and kiss the top of her head.

"I'm glad you're home." She presses her lips against my chest, and then her body relaxes into mine and her breath evens out, letting me know she's already fallen back asleep.

I close my eyes and smooth my fingers down her arm, knowing I won't be falling asleep anytime soon. Before her, I'd go to the gym or out on a run when I got home in order to work off any spare energy I had. But now, with her, I'm happy to just do this—hold her, feel her body against mine, and breathe in her scent until she finally wakes up. And I'm able to work out my energy in a much more satisfying way.

Suggestion 12

TELL YOUR MOM

CHRISSIE

With the Christmas tree lit just feet away and the sound of carols filling the house, I study my mom from my place at the island in her kitchen as she hums along to the music. If you asked me even a month ago how Christmas at my mom's would look, this is not the scene I would have envisioned.

"I need to talk to you about New Year's," she tells me as she brings a bowl of boiled potatoes to the counter and then grabs a masher from the drawer.

"Are you coming to my place?" I ask, wondering if I should invite her to Gaston's club to hang out with everyone before we all go back to my place to watch the fireworks and ring in the New Year. After I've told her about Gaston, of course—something I plan on doing today, especially after seeing how okay she seems to be.

"Sorry, honey, no; that's what I need to tell you. I'm actually going on a cruise, and I won't be home for New Year's Eve."

I blink, sure I heard her wrong. "Did you just say you're going on a cruise?"

"Yes. I leave the day before New Year's Eve, so I'll still be able to see your brother and Sam, who both thought it was great I was doing something for myself." She smiles, then adds, "I'm excited. The first stop is in Acapulco, and from what I've read online, the beaches there are beautiful."

"You're going on a cruise, and you told Chris before you told me?"

"Oh, stop." She laughs, knowing my brother and I still argue to this day about who she loves most. "I wanted to make sure he wouldn't be upset if I went, with him and Sam coming into town. And I've only had these plans a few days. I knew I'd tell you today."

"Are you going alone?"

"Yes." She smiles nervously. "The cruise caters to people who are traveling alone. They hold events and gatherings so you can meet new people, and if I don't feel comfortable going to those events, there's gambling, which is something I know I'll enjoy."

"Gambling?"

"There's a casino on the boat." Her face becomes animated. "I went to Vegas once when I was in my twenties, a little before I met your dad, and I had a great time. Plus, I was awesome at that red-ball, black-ball game."

I don't know what the red-ball, black-ball game is. I also don't know who the woman is standing in front of me. My mom has always frowned at even the mention of a cruise and has never even talked about gambling before.

"Who are you, and what have you done with my mother?" I question, and she laughs like I've never heard her laugh before.

"I told you, honey. I'm going to find my happy," she says, and I close my eyes briefly in relief. This is what I've wanted for her for months, and I feel overwhelmed with happiness that she's finally, *finally* taking steps to move past my dad. And seeing her happy lets me know that I can share that I am too.

"I have something to tell you."

"What?"

"I'm seeing someone. And, well . . . he's amazing."

"What?" she cries, her hands flying—including the one with the masher she's using, causing a spray of potatoes to fly across the room and splatter against the cupboard. "Why haven't you told me?"

I look away, trying to figure out how to tell her without making her feel bad.

"It's my fault," she says stiffly, and my throat gets tight when I hear the pain in her voice. "I . . . you didn't want to tell me because you were scared of how I would react."

"You weren't in a good place. I wanted to tell you; I just didn't know *how* to tell you. I'm sorry." I shift uncomfortably on the stool.

"You have nothing to be sorry about. If I wasn't acting like an idiot, you wouldn't have felt the need to keep this a secret. I'm sorry for making you feel like you couldn't trust me."

"You don't have anything to be sorry about either. I understood what you were going through. I'm just glad you're dealing with things better now." I reach across the space between us and clasp her hand.

"Your advice helped. I didn't realize how much having to hear about your dad was hurting me. After I told all our old friends to stop telling me what he was up to, I was able to stop being angry all the time."

"That was actually Gaston's advice," I say, giving her hand a squeeze before letting it go.

She tips her head to the side in confusion. "Gaston?"

"The guy I'm seeing—his name is Gaston."

"Like the villain in *Beauty and the Beast*?"

"Yeah." I laugh, not surprised that her reaction to his name is the same as mine was. "And get this: his dog's name is LeFou."

"I love it." She grins. "Gaston and LeFou." She shakes her head. "Perfect."

"Most people call him Gus, but I agree, I love his name," I say softly.

"Is he with his family today?" she asks, going back to mashing the potatoes.

"No, his dad passed away a few years ago, and his mom lives in Jersey and Florida, depending on the season. She's flying in for New Year's, but today, he's spending Christmas with his best friend, who's married and has a little girl."

"You're not seeing him today?"

I chew the inside of my cheek. "We spent last night and this morning together." My stomach clenches as vivid memories of how we spent last night and this morning fill my mind, and I have to physically shake my head to remove them. "Plus, I wanted to be here with you."

"You should invite him over," she suggests, looking around at the counters covered with food. "We have plenty, since you can't exactly buy Christmas dinner for two."

"Um . . ."

"At least invite him for dessert," she continues, reading my nervous expression. "I'd like to meet him."

"I'll send him a text." I give in, thinking Gaston probably won't want to drive over here, so I might have some time to come to terms with the two of them meeting.

"After you do that, I want to hear all about him."

"There's a lot to tell," I inform her absently while I find my cell phone in my purse.

"We have a lot of time," she says as I send him a quick text, telling him my mom would like to meet him—as in tonight—if he's up for it, but it's okay if he doesn't want to drive over here. I also send him the address so he can see how far away it is. Approximately one minute after I press send on the text, my cell rings. "Is that him?" Mom asks, and I nod, looking at his name on the screen and wondering why he can't be like every other guy and just send a text back. "Are you going to answer it?"

Without answering her question, I press the green button and put my phone to my ear. "Can't you be like every other person living in this century and text back instead of calling?"

"Sweetheart." He chuckles. "If I did that, I wouldn't be able to hear your voice."

"Yeah, but you'd still be able to answer my question. And just so you know, this isn't helping you prove you're not actually an alien," I say, and then my head flies up when I hear my mother start to laugh. I study her face, wondering how much she can hear.

"You're adorable, and the answer to your question is yes. What time should I be there?"

"Come whenever you want!" Mom shouts, and I groan. Apparently, she can hear everything, even him through the phone.

"I'll be there at five," Gaston responds, and I know he's smiling. "I might be there before, depending on traffic."

I look at the clock on the wall. "That's in less than an hour."

"Yeah," he agrees.

"Is Luke going to be upset that you're leaving so early? Have you even eaten yet?"

"No. And Luke won't give a shit." He laughs. "Are you nervous about me meeting your mom?"

"What do you think?"

"I think you worry too much."

"Whatever," I grumble, and he laughs again.

"All right, sweetheart. I'll let you go and send you a text if I feel like I have something to tell you."

"Liar." I smile. "Tell Luke and his wife hi for me."

"Will do, but just so you know, Luke and Cammy want to meet you. And Cammy said if it doesn't happen soon, she's going to just show up at your shop one day."

"She's welcome to come to the shop anytime, but we'll make dinner happen before New Year's if we can all find the time."

"Good," he agrees quietly. "Now enjoy your time with your mom, and I'll see you soon."

"See you soon," I agree happily before I hang up.

"He calls you *sweetheart*, and he actually calls," Mom states, and I find her grinning at me. "How long have you two been seeing each other?"

"Not long, just a few weeks. But it feels like a lot longer."

She nods, then asks, "What was that about him being an alien?"

"He's just not a normal guy, or not like any guy I've ever met before."

The skin around her eyes crinkles as she smiles, and she says softly, "I can't wait to meet him, or hear all about him, so start talking, honey. And while you do that, put the rolls on a pan." She tips her head to the orange bag of rolls on the counter.

I fake pout. "I thought you were cooking for me?"

"I did." She waves her hands around at all the food she's cooked. "But now I'm going to need your help so I can make a good impression on Gaston. So turn the oven back on so we can heat stuff up, and talk fast, because I want to know everything about your guy before he gets here."

"So bossy." I get off the stool I planted myself on when I got here and walk around the kitchen island. As soon as I'm close to my mom, I kiss the side of her head, and she smiles as her bottom lip wobbles. I ignore the wobble and get to work while telling her everything that's mom appropriate about Gaston, and I tell her quickly, because he's going to be here soon. Really soon.

With the table set, and the food that needed to be heated back up warmed and waiting for us to dig in, I watch Gaston pull into my mom's driveway with my stomach in knots.

"Is he here?" Mom asks as she pulls the ham from the oven and carries it to the table.

"Yes." I start toward the back door but stop and turn to look at her. "Please be on your best behavior."

Her brows come together. "Since when am I not on my best behavior?"

"I don't know." I raise my hands in the air. "Since when do you decide on a whim to go on a cruise and admit you enjoy gambling?"

"Right." She laughs. "I promise I'll be on my best behavior." She crosses her heart. "Now, go get your guy."

I let out a breath, open the door, and head down the steps as Gaston gets out of his car, holding a bouquet of flowers. When I see them, my nervousness starts to slide away and my heart warms.

"Hey," I say softly once we're toe to toe, and he grins as he captures me behind my neck with his free hand and tips his head down as I lean up and touch my mouth to his.

When his lips leave mine and my eyes open, I find him studying me. "You okay with this?"

"Yes." I rest my hands against his abs. "I'm a little nervous, but I want you two to meet."

"It's going to be all good."

"I know." I look at the flowers and then him and raise a brow. "How did you manage to get flowers on Christmas Day?"

"Cammy." He smirks, looking pleased with himself. "She bought three bouquets for the table, so I asked if I could have one to give to your mom."

"You really are an overachiever. You know that, right?"

He chuckles, kissing my forehead, and then turns me into his side, wrapping his arm around my shoulders. "I just want to make a good impression."

"Like you could ever make a bad impression." I wrap my arm around his back and walk up the driveway. When we reach the back door, I step into the house before him and find my mom trying to pretend like she hasn't been looking out the window since I walked outside.

Her eyes smile as she takes in Gaston and the flowers he's holding, and she comes toward us.

"Mom, this is Gaston. Gaston, my mom, Dorothy."

"Nice to meet you, ma'am." He bends to kiss her cheek; then he passes her the flowers when he leans back.

"You too." Mom's smile is so big I'm afraid her face might crack. "Thank you for these. That's very sweet of you. I hope you're hungry."

"Starved." His hand finds mine, and he gives my fingers an affectionate squeeze.

"Honey, take Gaston and get settled at the table. I'm going to put these in water and get our drinks."

"I can help," I tell her.

"I got it." She waves me off. "What would you like, Gus? I have tea, wine, and I might even have a beer somewhere in the back of the fridge."

"Tea is fine," Gaston tells her, and she nods, then looks at me. "Wine?"

"Yes, please. Thanks, Mom."

"No problem. Go get seated. I'll be there in just a minute."

I lead Gaston to the table and smile as he holds out my chair before sitting next to me. I look at the table and my mom's place setting at the head of the table, feeling a little melancholy all of a sudden. I haven't reached out to my father since our run-in at the grocery store, and I honestly don't know if I will. But this moment, with Gaston meeting my mom, makes me wish things were different—that my dad was meeting him too, that my parents were still together, and that I would get to experience them sitting down to a meal with the man I'm pretty sure I'm in love with. It's sad I will never get to experience that, and heartbreaking when I think about having kids one day and them maybe not ever having a relationship with their grandfather.

"You okay, baby?"

Gaston's question pulls me from my thoughts, and I turn my head to look at him. "Yeah, just thinking about my dad." I shrug, and his expression turns stormy. Even with him encouraging me to reach out to my dad, he's pissed that my father hasn't tried to contact me. If I'm honest, I'm pissed at him too. I feel like if he cared about me at all, he would have called to make sure I was okay and to see when we could meet to talk about things.

"Fuck," Gaston growls angrily, and I know I shouldn't have said anything.

"I'm fine. Just ignore me." I pat his thigh, and his eyes narrow on mine. "Seriously, I'm fine."

"You're not fine." He shakes his head, not looking any less pissed.

"Okay, you're right. I'm not. But it's Christmas, and I don't want my mom upset."

"Right." His jaw ticks, and I watch him force his body to relax as my mom comes to the table, handing him his glass of tea, and he thanks her before she leaves again. "It will be okay." He leans over, kissing the side of my head, and I nod as my mom comes back in holding two glasses of wine.

"Let's eat." She hands me my glass, then starts to uncover the dishes. I reach for the plate with the ham on it and take two pieces, putting them on Gaston's plate before taking a piece for myself.

"He's very handsome," Mom says under her breath as she hands me the basket of rolls.

"He is, and he can also hear you," I point out, and her eyes fly to Gaston, who I hear laugh as he gives my thigh a warm, reassuring squeeze under the table.

"You're very handsome," she informs him.

"Thank you, Dorothy." I hear the humor in his tone.

"I hope, with you in my daughter's life, she'll finally do what she told me she was going to do weeks ago and hire someone to help her out so she can stop working so much and start having fun again."

"Mom," I warn her.

Not surprisingly, she ignores me and continues talking to Gaston like I'm not even here while placing a scoop of mashed potatoes on her plate before passing me the bowl.

"I don't know why she hasn't hired someone to help her already. Her bakery has been thriving since it opened." She glances proudly in my direction as I put mashed potatoes on both our plates. "She's even been written up in the paper a few times and won a couple awards for local businesses."

"Really?" Gus asks, and I turn my head to meet his gaze over my shoulder.

"It's really not that big of a deal. There's only a few other bakeries in the area—"

"It's a big deal," Mom cuts in, and my eyes go to her. "You won first place two years in a row. The businesses you were up against are established in this area. They have been here for *years*, and you still beat them by a landslide."

"I didn't beat them." I shake my head as I motion to the green bean casserole and silently ask if Gus wants some, and when he nods, I place a scoop on his plate. "It wasn't even a competition. It was just a few people from the area who voted for their favorite places to eat or get a cookie and a cup of coffee."

"As you can see, my daughter is oblivious to her talent," Mom states with an annoyed sigh.

"I'm seeing that," Gaston agrees with quiet warmth, making me want to kiss him.

With my mom present, I ignore that urge and pin her in place with a look.

"Well," I say sassily, "you'll be happy to know I have an ad going out in the paper and online this weekend, and I plan on posting a help wanted ad on the window of the shop after I open back up. Hopefully, with that, I'll get some inquiries and be able to hire someone full time before the New Year."

"Maybe your Gus *is* an alien," Mom mumbles to me with wide, surprised eyes, and he laughs before clearing his throat.

"Your daughter is a smart woman," Gus says, gaining my mom's attention, and I watch her eyes soften before I turn to look at him as he continues to speak. "As the owner of three businesses—a club I purchased straight out, and two bars that I acquired after they went belly-up—I only respect her more for not taking on more than she knew she could handle." His expression fills with pride as his fingers around the top of my thigh tighten in a comforting gesture. "I agree even more after what you've just said that she could, and can, hire someone full time to help, but I respect that she's followed her gut and taken things slow. A lot of people get caught up in momentary success and assume things will keep growing for them. Not always, but on occasion, that doesn't happen, and when it does, they're left trying to figure out how to pay their employees, along with all their other expenses. In the end, they end up losing all they've built."

"I never thought of it like that," Mom says quietly with respect in her tone, and I find her looking at me with a whole new light in her eyes. "Obviously, you know what you're doing, but as your mom, you have to understand I want what's best for you. Not financially, but emotionally."

"I know," I tell her, and she reaches out with her hand, capturing mine on the table, and then she leans toward me, kissing the side of my head.

My eyes close as I soak up the feeling of her approval and attention. When I open my eyes, she's smiling with pride.

"You've always been smart, honey." She pats my hand, then eyes Gus briefly. "I'm just happy to see you've found a guy who sees just how smart you are."

I should feel embarrassed by my mother's observation, but as Gaston's hand finds mine and he links our fingers together, I feel nothing but contentment. The rest of the evening progresses without any more deep conversations, and by the time the night comes to an end and I watch my guy kiss my mom's cheek in goodbye, I'm actually happy the two of them met, and I'm even more happy they seem to get along.

"Thank you again for dinner," Gaston says.

Mom pats his arm while she tips her head back to look up at him. "You're welcome at my table anytime." She lets him go, then comes to me with her arms open and a smile on her face. "I love you, honey." Her arms engulf me, and then she whispers, "I'm so happy for you, and he really is amazing."

"I know," I whisper back, holding on to her a little tighter before letting her go. "I'll see you in a few days, when Chris and Sam get here, right?"

"You will." She kisses my cheek, then walks me to Gaston, who leads me to my car and opens the door. I wave at her as Gaston gets into his own car, which is parked next to mine, and then we both back out of the driveway, him following me as we drive the twenty minutes home.

When we arrive at our building, he drives past me to park in the exclusive indoor parking that is only available to those who live on his floor and the one below, and I park in my outdoor space. I get out of my car and start toward the lobby, and he comes out to meet me halfway, looking a little annoyed.

"What?"

"I'm going to move my bike to my club and park it in the storage unit there so you can park your car in my second space. I don't like that you're parking out here at night," he grumbles, taking my bag, then grabbing my hand.

"I've been living here for over a year and a half. I don't mind parking out here, and it's not like I'm walking a mile in the dark through the ghetto to get into the building," I tell him, and he glances down at me, not looking any happier.

"I don't like that you have to walk through this parking lot at all, and since I have the ability to do something to change it, that's what I'm going to do."

"What if I said I don't want that?" I ask.

"I'd say too bad."

"How did I know that would be your answer?" I mutter, and his hand around mine tightens.

"I want to know you're safe, even if it's just making it so you're able to drive under the building and get into an elevator instead of walking across a dark parking lot."

"You know I shouldn't like that you are so overprotective, right?" I look up at him as we enter the lobby hand in hand. "I think it's written somewhere that a woman nowadays should be independent and self-reliant, that she shouldn't look for a man to keep her safe."

"Whoever said that was an idiot." He presses the button for the elevator when we reach it, and when the doors open, he tugs me inside and hits the button for his floor, then presses me against the wall. "I don't care if you don't need to be taken care of because you're an independent woman. I'm going to take care of you anyway, in all the ways I can."

I shouldn't love his words, but I still do. Like everything with him since the moment we met, I'm thankful he is who he is. He makes me feel safe, he makes me feel at peace, and he makes me feel cherished and wanted. I don't think I could have found a better guy if I was looking for one, and I'm pretty sure I've gone from falling in love to *being* in love with him.

Suggestion 13

Breathe through the Goodness

CHRISSIE

I fall back to the kitchen counter, my fingers curving tightly around the edge as I lift my legs higher around Gaston's hips, moaning, "God, please don't stop." I feel the tension in my lower belly start to unravel as my vision dims with the force of the orgasm that's coming on quickly.

"Give it to me," he orders, circling my clit, and I let go. My body tingles from my scalp down to my toes as my inner walls contract around him. He continues his ruthless thrusts while manipulating my clit, and my orgasm spirals out of control. I absently hear him groan as his thrusts slow, but my mind and body disintegrate as I continue to come.

Completely lost in the feel of his heavy weight settling against me while he kisses the side of my neck, I wrap my arms around him tightly, whispering "I think I love you" into his skin. When my mind registers his muscles bunching under my palms, I realize what I just said and squeeze my eyes closed.

Oh goodness. There's a huge difference between saying "I think I love you" to him and admitting to myself I'm falling in love. What was I thinking? Oh yeah, I wasn't thinking at all. My mind was in Gaston heaven.

"What?" He pulls back, and my eyes open while my hold on him loosens.

"What?" I repeat as his gaze holds mine hostage.

"What did you say?" Every muscle in my body gets tight while the breath in my lungs gets trapped there. "Chrissie." My name is filled with warning.

I attempt to play dumb, even with my mind still partly mush and my body still floating on the high of my orgasms. "Did I say something?"

"You did." His expression softens while he slides his arms under my back and lifts me up to face him, causing my breath to catch as he slides impossibly deeper. "You think you love me."

"What? Why would you say that?"

"Because the words 'I think I love you' came out of your mouth not even a minute ago," he answers, with a small smile forming on his lips.

"Cock," I blurt, placing my hands against his warm chest, and his head jerks back.

"Pardon?"

"I think I love your cock." I nod my head, a little proud of myself for coming up with that on a whim. "You missed the words 'your cock.'"

He grins, and there's something about it that's a little scary, but before I can figure out what it is about his look that sets me on edge, he lifts me off the counter and starts toward his bedroom.

"Gus . . ."

"Quiet," he demands.

My eyes widen, and my heart starts to pound; then, before I have time to prepare for the loss of him, he releases me suddenly and I fall backward, bouncing against the mattress. "What are you doing? I have to get ready . . ." The words *for work* get lost as he comes down over me, kissing me deeply and turning me on all over again with one kiss.

He drags his mouth from mine, then trails his lips to my breast, licking over my nipple before sucking it into his mouth. My body arches and my fingers slide through his hair as I silently beg him to continue. When he pulls away once more, my lashes flutter open.

"If you can't say it again without coming, I'll make you come over and over until you tell me what you said."

I keep my mouth closed, and he grins his scary grin once more before moving to my other breast. I do everything I can to control my body's reaction to him as he manipulates both my breasts with his mouth, teeth, and tongue, and I succeed until he skillfully slides his hand between my legs. The moment he zeros in on my clit with his thumb and thrusts two fingers inside me, I cry out his name and get lost on the waves of euphoria building deep within me. With nothing else to do, I hold on to him, digging my nails into his skin and whimpering into his mouth as he kisses me.

"Tell me what you said." The words are growled against my lips, and I jerk my head from side to side—not in denial of his request but in shock as the walls of my pussy start to convulse and I come. His fingers slow their invasion, but they never stop completely, which means one orgasm becomes another. He doesn't give me a chance to recover from another world-altering climax; he settles himself between my legs and thrusts into me hard.

I moan, wrapping myself around him, and breathe, "I can't. It's too much."

"Tell me what you said." He circles my oversensitive clit, and I shake my head and close my eyes as my pussy ripples around his cock.

"Gus," I whisper, overwhelmed. It feels like every inch of me is on fire.

"Look at me."

My lashes flutter open again. I stare into his eyes and see warmth, devotion, and happiness looking back at me. A sense of peace and rightness washes through every cell in my body, and I lean up, placing my lips against his. I tell him the truth, knowing down to my soul that he can handle it. "I think I'm in love with you."

"Thank God," he hisses, right before he captures my mouth and links our hands together, lifting them over my head. His weight settles heavily on me, and his thrusts turn lazy and slow as he slides in and out. I hold him with my legs around his hips, and we come simultaneously, clinging to one another until the waves of ecstasy begin to fade away.

With both of us breathing heavily and my heart beating so hard it feels like it might come right out of my chest, he lifts up, holding his body above mine with my hands still captured in his grasp against the bed. "I don't *think* I love you, sweetheart. I just straight up love you."

His words cause overwhelming happiness to bubble up from within me, and I force him to let me go, then wrap my arms around him while shoving my face into his neck. Tears I can't hold back fill my eyes, and a quiet sob slides up the back of my throat.

"Don't cry," he whispers, peppering soft kisses on my chest and neck, then cheeks and lips. I fight back my tears and attempt to focus on his handsome face, not quite believing this guy is mine.

"You love me?" I sniffle.

"Yes," he says softly as his fingers move along the side of my face.

"I love you too," I admit, and his expression fills with tenderness. I lose his look as he lowers his head, but I feel it as he kisses me, which is even better.

"I wish you didn't have to go to work," he grates out, annoyed, pulling away to rest his forehead against mine.

"I know," I agree, sounding out of breath and just as frustrated as him.

"I understand why you're being choosy, but you need to hire someone, sweetheart."

"I know." I feel a little off balance as he rolls us until I'm resting fully against his chest, suddenly looking down at him. "It's only been two days since Christmas, and I know I'm being picky, but I'm waiting for the right person to come in."

At my statement, his features fill with understanding. "You'll find them." His hands span my waist and he sits up, taking me with him. "Wanna shower?"

"Yes." I smile, and then with his alien strength, he maneuvers us both out of bed and carries me to the bathroom. Surprisingly, I'm not late opening the shop, but I honestly wouldn't care if I were. Finding out Gaston is in love with me is worth a whole lot more than a few paying customers.

With Aubrey and Rachelle out picking us up lunch, I'm surprised when I hear a soft, sweet, southern voice call "Hello!" from the front of the shop. I didn't hear the chime on the door ring, letting me know someone walked in, so either the chime is broken, or I was really focused on what I was doing and lost in thought. With Gaston and what happened this morning constantly filling my mind, and the last couple of days being so busy, it was probably the latter.

"Be right there!" I shout, walking to the sink to wash the icing off my fingers, and I hear "Okay!" called back. I grab a paper towel once I turn off the water and dry my hands as I go through the open door and out into the main shop.

"Can I help you?" I ask the top of the coppery-red hair that's bent looking into one of the two display cases. At my question, the woman's head comes up, and I am momentarily stunned by her large green eyes and elegant, freckled features. She looks like a real-life fairy princess.

"Hi, I'm Anna Bell. I'm looking for"—she drops her eyes and looks at her phone in her hand—"the owner, Chrissie."

"That's me." I smile, and when she smiles back, I notice a slight gap between her two front teeth that makes her look even more endearing. "How can I help you?"

"I'm here to apply for the job that was in the paper."

"Great, do you mind if we talk out there?" I incline my head toward the tables out front.

"Not at all."

"Awesome." I grab my notebook, along with a can of Coke. "Would you like something to drink or eat while we chat?"

"That's sweet, but no, thank you. I just had a huge lunch at a restaurant down the block." She pats her stomach.

"The Grill?" I ask, and when she nods, I laugh. "That is one of my favorite places to eat, and I always leave regretting my decision to go there, because the food is so good I can't stop eating, even when I know I'm full."

"I'm suffering that fate now." She giggles as I walk out from behind the counter and across the shop to one of the tables near the window, chanting in my head, *I hope you're the one*. I haven't put a notice up in the window of the shop. I haven't needed to. Since the day after my ad went live in the paper and online, I've been interviewing people left and right. But so far, not one person has felt right for the job, even with most applicants being highly qualified. Like I told Gaston this morning, I know I might be being too picky, but if I'm going to do this, I want the best person possible helping me run my business.

As soon as we both sit, without a word she hands me a few sheets of paper stapled together, and I flip through them. I look over her résumé and work history, a little surprised and worried that she's applying for a job here and not downtown at one of the big law firms or corporate buildings. Most of her previous work history involves clerical or secretarial work, not baking or even retail.

"Can I ask why you're applying for this job?" I lift my head to look at her.

"As you can see, I've worked in corporate my entire adult life. I did it because it was what I went to school for and what I was *supposed* to do."

"You didn't enjoy it?" I surmise, and she shakes her head.

"I hated every minute of it." She leans forward. "Can I be honest with you?" Considering what she just said, I thought we were already being honest, so I nod. "I just want to be happy," she whispers, and my heart clenches in my chest at her tone and the look in her eyes. "A little over a year ago, I left the man I was supposed to spend the rest of my life with, and a month ago, I moved here on a whim, needing to be closer to the ocean. I don't know what I'm doing." She looks away briefly, seeming contemplative. "I do know"—her gaze comes back to me—"I have always loved baking and cooking. I also know how to manage people and my time, and I'm a quick study. I'm sure, looking over my résumé, you can see I'm probably the least-experienced person for this job, but when I saw the ad, I knew I had to apply and that I'd regret it if I didn't."

Her words touch something deep within me, and I study her for a long moment before I speak. "The hours are not set in stone. Sometimes I'd need you here to open early, and other days I'd need you to close. Would you be okay with that?"

"Can I drink coffee on the job and eat a cookie or cupcake whenever I want?"

"Yes."

"Then I think I'd be okay with that," she agrees with a soft smile.

Not wanting her to think this will be all cupcakes and sprinkles, pun intended, I tell her, "My two part-time shop girls are both leaving at the end of summer, and until I can hire replacements for them, things might be a little crazier than normal."

"I thrive on crazy," she says, and hope blooms in my chest.

"You also might have to work on your own from time to time, depending on the day."

"If I can handle lawyers and CEOs breathing down my neck day in and day out, I think I can handle that."

"When can you start?" I ask, surprising even myself.

She sits back, seeming stunned, and then states with happiness in her eyes, "Today? Tomorrow? Really, I'm open to anything."

"All right, why don't you come in tomorrow morning at nine? We can see how things go and if this is the right fit for both of us." I stop, then add, "I'll of course pay you for the day, even if you decide this isn't for you."

"Really?"

"Really." I nod, and I think she might cry, but she pulls in a breath, and when she releases it I can see she's got the urge under control.

"Thank you."

"Don't thank me yet." I smile. "You might find out tomorrow that you hate it here and wish you'd never applied."

"I don't see that happening." She laughs.

"Me neither," I agree, feeling hopeful.

I look over her shoulder as the chime for the door rings, letting me know it's not broken, and I feel my stomach melt as I watch Gaston search for me when he steps inside the shop.

When his eyes land on mine, I smile and scoot back from the table to stand, and then I look down at Anna, whose eyes are pointed over her shoulder. "Thank you for coming in. I'll see you tomorrow at nine," I say, and Anna jumps, pulling her eyes off Gaston to look at me, and gets up quickly.

"Nine. Right. I'll be here," she repeats, and I almost laugh. I'm not at all surprised that she's been swiftly sucked into the vortex of Gaston's hotness, but I'm silently thrilled he hasn't even spared the gorgeous woman more than a casual glance.

As I walk toward my guy, she starts for the door at my side, and I stop her to make introductions. "Anna, this is Gus." I glance from her to him. "Gus, this is Anna. She's coming in tomorrow to see if she'll like working here." A look of relief crosses his face before he tips his head down and holds out his hand toward her.

Her cheeks get pink as she reaches out to shake his hand, and her words are mumbled as she says, "Nice to meet you," making me fight back laughter.

"You too." Gus lets her hand go to capture me possessively around the waist, and she gives me an awkward smile before she leaves through the door.

I watch her walk past the windows looking dazed, and I shake my head, and then I tip my head back toward Gus, and his gaze dips to meet mine. "I think for the sake of business and my shop girls' sanity, I should ban you from my bakery." At my comment, his fingers curl tightly around the side of my waist, and he lowers his head so he can touch his smiling lips to mine. "I'm not kidding," I inform him when he pulls slightly away. "My girls can't handle being in your presence without going all awkward. It's not good for business."

"They'll get over it," he informs me, still smiling.

"I don't think they will." I shake my head in denial. "Aubrey is better than Rachelle at keeping her giddiness locked away whenever you come into the shop, but the two of them still fumble around like newborn baby deer whenever you're here." I narrow my eyes on his in mock annoyance. "I don't even want to imagine the kind of destruction you leave behind whenever you enter your club or one of your bars."

He laughs at my joke, but I catch the somewhat guarded look in his eyes. I start to open my mouth to ask him what that's about, but before I can get a word out, he distracts me with a deep kiss that makes my toes curl and my mind blank of anything but him.

"What are we doing for dinner?" he asks, holding me tightly while keeping his mouth close to mine.

I attempt to catch my breath and blink away the haze of desire that has settled over me and admit, "I don't know."

"I was on my way to the store; that's why I stopped by. I wanted to see what you're in the mood for."

Him holding me so tightly and speaking with his lips brushing mine, I tell him the truth. "I just want you."

"You've got me." He brushes his lips across mine. "So what do you want to eat?"

"I can cook." I rest my hands against his chest, and he lifts one brow. "Don't give me that look. I can cook more than breakfast, even if I haven't done it yet."

"So you've said, but I have yet to experience you cooking dinner for me." He chuckles.

"Whatever." I laugh, shoving against his chest gently, and he covers my hands with his, holding them against his shirt. "Fine, I won't cook, because it's going to be late by the time I leave here, but I can pick something up on my way home." I lean slightly into him. "I know you're busy with getting things ready for New Year's."

"I don't mind cooking, and since you don't know what you want, I'll surprise you."

"You really don't have to make me dinner," I repeat, feeling guilty that he's working so hard and still taking care of me.

"I know I don't, but I'm still going to." He kisses me swiftly, then lets me go when the door chimes and Aubrey and Rachelle walk in carrying bags of food, and they both smile when they see us together.

"Hi, Gus," Aubrey stops to say, and Rachelle, who's staring at Gus, runs right into her friend's back, almost knocking her over.

"Sorry." Rachelle laughs, then smiles at Gus. "Hey."

"See?" I roll my eyes, hearing Gaston chuckle.

"Hey, girls," he says to the two of them, and then he looks down at me. "I'll see you tonight, baby."

"See you tonight." I walk him to the door, receiving one more kiss before he walks out. Once he's gone, I turn to face my girls, who are both grinning at me. "What?"

"You're so totally in love with him." Aubrey points at me.

"And he's totally in love with you." Rachelle grins.

"You're both right," I say, and they let out loud, earsplitting, girly screeches before they do their normal jumping-around business. I watch the two of them celebrate my newfound love and happiness, and I force myself to breathe through the goodness when I really want to cry happy tears.

Suggestion 14

LAY THE GROUNDWORK

GASTON

I walk with LeFou on his leash to where Chrissie is standing just outside the lobby doors of our building, and her head turns at our approach. Seeing the excited look on her face, I shake my head, saying softly, "Sweetheart, you need to relax."

"I can't." She bounces on her toes, and LeFou at her feet hops up on his hind legs to join her in her excitement. When his front paws make contact with her shins, she pauses long enough to pick him up, then cuddles him against her chest and tells me something I already know. "They're going to be here any minute."

I study her beautiful face filled with happiness, not surprised I feel the way I do about her in such a short amount of time. This woman has given me something I wasn't exactly looking for, and there is no denying I'm crazy in love with her.

"I just can't wait for you to meet Chris and Sam, and for them to meet you."

At her quiet statement, I wrap my hand around her hip and bring her a step closer to me. "You're not nervous." It's a statement, not a question, and she sags against me.

"No, Chris and Sam already know all about you, so I don't have anything to be nervous about."

I know this is true, since her brother calls her often in the evenings when I'm around, and she's never been anything but honest with him about our relationship. The situation with her father is a completely different story. She hasn't told anyone but Leah and me that she even ran into him, and she's dealt with the whole situation by not dealing with it at all—something that, in the long run, is going to fester into an ugly wound. My hope is that while her brother is here, she'll tell him about seeing their father, and they can go speak to him together.

"Have you thought any more about what I said this morning? About talking to your brother about your dad?"

"Yeah."

"And?"

"I'm going to talk to him," she says with pain lacing her words as she drops her forehead to the center of my chest, with LeFou wiggling between us. I slide my fingers through the hair at the back of her skull, then bend forward and kiss the top of her head, lifting my eyes when a car pulls up.

Seeing it's a taxi, I tell her quietly, "They're here."

"Finally." She lifts her forehead off my chest, quickly standing up on her tiptoes to kiss me. Once she falls back to her flat feet, she grabs my hand and orders, "Come on," dragging me with her toward the taxi as the back doors open.

As soon as her brother—who looks just like her, except a little taller, with a beard covering the lower half of his face—gets out, she lets me go so she can run toward him at full speed, still holding on to LeFou. I stop as they embrace, then laugh as LeFou starts to yelp in excitement and wiggles to join in on their reunion with doggie kisses.

Chrissie's laughter fills the air as her brother lets her go so he can take hold of the wild pup trying to climb up his chest. He states to

LeFou, "You're even cuter in person," holding him up and away to study him.

"And he's hotter," I hear muttered.

I turn to find a man, who I know is Sam from the photos I've seen around Chrissie's place, smiling at her while he pays the cabdriver. Where Chris is short and bulky, Sam is tall and slim, with blond, almost white, hair and blue eyes. Chrissie laughs at Sam's observation, then runs to him, throwing her arms around his neck, and he picks her up to swing her around.

"Hey, kid, I see you didn't mess around when finding a hot guy," he says when he drops her to her feet, and she grins at him before she turns and forces herself under his arm.

"Ignore him. I promise he's harmless," Chris says, setting LeFou on the ground, then stepping toward me. "It's nice to finally meet you."

"You too." I give his hand a shake as Chrissie pulls Sam toward us.

"Gus, this is Sam," she tells me, and I grin at her, then look at Sam.

"Nice to meet you, man."

"You too." He reaches out to give my arm a squeeze, and then he looks at Chrissie, saying, "Seriously, nice job," and she giggles.

"This is what I have to deal with anytime these two get together," Chris tells me, and then he narrows his eyes on his guy and his sister. "Can you two work at not making Gus uncomfortable?"

"Gus doesn't get uncomfortable. He doesn't even understand the effect he has on people, especially women," Chrissie says, and Sam chuckles.

"This is why I live hundreds of miles away," Chris tells me, and then he looks at his sister. "Can we get our bags and go inside?"

"Of course." She laughs, and Chris rolls his eyes before he goes to grab his bag, and Sam does the same. I reach out for Chrissie's hand and head into the building and to the elevator.

"How long before we're meeting Mom for dinner?" Chris asks when we get upstairs to Chrissie's place, and she pulls her cell phone out of her pocket to look at it.

"Just about three hours," she says while leading both men pulling their suitcases toward her bedroom, where they'll be staying while they're here in town. Before Dorothy decided to go away for New Year's, the plan was for them to stay with her. But with her leaving, I thought it would be better if they were close to Chrissie, so I convinced her to stay with me and give them her place. At first she wasn't sure, not with my mom staying with me. But after some convincing and explaining, I got her to agree, even if she's not a hundred percent on board.

Hopefully, she'll feel more comfortable after she meets my mom tomorrow, and if she's not, she'll still be okay. My mom won't be around much. Even with only coming to see me once a year for the last five years that I've lived here, she's met people and made friends she likes to visit with while she's in town. Plus, she is the kind of person who is always busy, always on the go. And Chrissie also has her brother and Sam here to spend time with.

"Anyone want a beer?" I call out and get two yeses and one "Wine, please" as I head for the kitchen and unhook LeFou from his leash. The moment he's free, he takes off to find a place to hang out, and I go to the fridge. I pour a glass of wine for Chrissie first, then grab three beers and pop the tops off. I take a seat on the couch in the living room, and a few minutes later, my woman comes out to join me and falls onto the couch at my side. I lean forward to grab her glass of wine and hand it to her, then ask, "You happy?"

"Yes." She puts the glass to her lips and takes a sip before she places her feet up on the couch and leans into me. I lift my arm, making room for her, and she curls against my side with a happy sigh as her brother and Sam come into the living room, both grabbing their beers from the coffee table.

"Have you talked to Dad?" Chris asks as he and Sam take a seat in the double chair that's catty-corner to the couch, and Chrissie's weight against me goes completely still.

"What?"

"I don't know," her brother says. "I thought he might have reached out to you to tell you Merry Christmas."

"He hasn't," she says. "Did he reach out to you?"

At her question, Chris shakes his head.

"Sweetheart," I prompt, and she looks up at me. "Tell them," I order, and she frowns, then lets out a frustrated sigh when she sees I'm not going to give in.

"What happened? Is Mom okay?" Chris asks, looking between us and sounding concerned.

"Mom's fine." She takes a sip of wine. "Actually, I think she's better than she's ever been."

"Dad?" Chris asks with his jaw ticking.

"Yes." She ducks her head. "I mean, I'm sure he's fine too. It's just that I ran into him a little while back."

"You did?" He frowns, studying her averted face. "You never told me you saw him."

"I know." She sighs.

"Let me guess. You weren't going to tell me, because you didn't want me upset, just like you didn't want us to tell Mom about Dad not talking to us for the same reason."

"You can't be mad that I don't want the people I love upset."

"No, but I can be pissed at you for keeping secrets from me. Now tell me what happened."

"He was with his wife at the grocery store," she says, taking a sip of wine.

"And?" he asks, sounding frustrated.

With a heavy sigh, she tells him what went down, and when she's done, he doesn't look any happier than he did. In fact, he looks pissed, and so does Sam.

"So he didn't call you after that bullshit?" Sam grates out after a moment, and Chrissie looks to him, shaking her head.

"I just cannot believe him," Chris rumbles, standing up, obviously too pissed off to sit any longer. "First, he just . . . fuck, you know what he did." He glances at his sister. "Then, after he runs into you with his new wife in the grocery store and you freak out, he doesn't even have the decency to call you and make sure you're okay?"

"I haven't called him either," Chrissie whispers, and Chris's eyes move to her in a flash and narrow.

"He's your dad, *our* fucking dad. I don't give a fuck what is going on in his head. He should have fucking called you. He should have phoned you to check in, even if it was just to make sure you got home okay. Jesus," he clips, running his fingers through his hair. He tips his head back toward the ceiling. "I don't even know him, and now I wonder if I ever did."

"Chris," Sam calls out, and Chris's head lowers. His eyes go to Sam's. Neither of them says a word, but I know they're still communicating something between each other, and I have to admit it's beautiful to watch that kind of deep understanding.

When Chris pulls his eyes away from Sam, he looks at his sister, and his expression softens. "I'm sorry you had to deal with that. I fucking hate that you had to see them together." He looks from Chrissie to me. "Thank you for being there for her when that went down."

I lift my chin, then tell him the same thing I've been telling his sister. "I think you and Chrissie should reach out to your father while you're here and ask him to meet up. You both deserve to understand why he did what he did, and I hope when it's done, everyone can move on, or at least things won't be so awkward if your sister runs into him or his wife again."

147

"I'll make that happen." He steps toward the couch and his sister, and then he pulls her up to stand and gives her a hug. "We'll get this sorted," he tells her, and she buries her face in his chest before wrapping her arms around his back to cling to him.

I look at Sam, who's watching them with a somber expression. He feels my gaze, and his eyes come to me, and he gives me a sad smile. He's been dealing with this situation from the beginning, right along with Chris and Chrissie, so I have no doubt he's just as confused about everything that has occurred with their father as they are.

I pull Chrissie down to my lap when her brother lets her go, and she tucks her face against my neck and wraps her arms around my waist as she cries quietly. I try to remember it's good she's letting this shit out and not holding it in, even though I really hate her tears. After some time, she pulls her face back to look at me, then closes her eyes and drops her forehead to the center of my chest as her bottom lip wobbles. "I love you."

Jesus, I don't know if I will ever get used to hearing those words come out of her mouth.

"Love you too." I kiss the top of her head, then look up to find Chris and Sam both studying us with the same warm expressions.

"We have happy news," Sam says as he reaches over to take Chris's hand, and Chrissie lifts her head to look at the two of them.

"What news?" she asks, wiping her cheeks and scooting off my lap.

"We're getting married."

"What?" she yells, and I barely have time to prepare for her sudden movement as she launches herself at both men. "Oh my God. Why didn't you say anything before now?"

"We wanted to tell you in person," Sam says, giving Chris a look, and her brother rolls his eyes at him.

"When did this happen, and who asked who?" she questions, looking between the two of them.

"Neither of us asked," Chris replies with softness filling his voice. "We were talking about our plan to adopt a child and then about names, and we knew we'd want our baby and us to all have the same last name. So getting married was just an obvious step. Well, that and I am tired of calling him my partner, like we're playing a game of chess." He grins.

"Wait." Chrissie shakes her head. "You guys are getting married and having a baby?"

"Yes, but we aren't having a big wedding, since we need to save for the adoption process. And who knows how long it will take for us to get chosen by a birth mother? The agency we found says it takes a year for the average couple to have a child placed with them, and since we're not average, we know we might have to wait awhile. We'd like to get the ball rolling sooner than later, which means when we get home, we'll file for a marriage license. And once that's approved, we'll make it official and move on to the next step."

"This is such amazing news. I'm so happy for both of you." She hugs her brother and Sam before asking, "Have you told Mom yet?"

"No, we were going to share the news at dinner, but apparently Sam needed you to stop looking so depressed, so he decided to tell you now," Chris says, giving Sam an unhappy look, and Sam shrugs.

"Dinner," Chrissie whispers, then she looks at me. "What time is it?"

I glance at the watch on my wrist. "Five."

"Oh crap." She bolts up off the couch and looks down at me. "I have to go fix my face."

"You look beautiful."

"I look like I've been crying, and my mom is a dog with a bone when she wants to know something. And she has no idea we haven't talked to our dad, and I don't want her to know that, especially with her leaving tomorrow to go on vacation."

"Right," I mutter, then stand and look between Sam and Chris. "We'll be back down to pick you both up for dinner, unless you two want to come up and hang at my place until it's time to go."

"We're good here. I wanna shower, and Sam is going to snooze," Chris says, then looks at his sister. "I'm going to send Dad a message and see if he's open to meeting with us."

"Okay," she agrees, not sounding happy about the idea.

He stands and looks down at her, taking hold of her face and telling her softly, "This whole thing isn't yours to deal with on your own, and you have people who love you and want to be here for you, so let us."

"I'm going to try," she says.

Chris looks at me. "Word of warning: she always thinks she needs to protect everyone, even if it means hurting herself, and you will never be able to convince her that you don't need protecting."

"Whatever, we need to go," Chrissie mutters, then tips her head back toward me. "Are you ready?"

"Yeah, baby." I place my hand against her lower back and lead her to the door, where she already has her overnight bag waiting. I take it from her when she picks it up, then take her up to my place. And since I'm not one to miss an opportunity, I jump in the shower with her, where we spend more time than we should before we get ready for dinner with her family.

Suggestion 15

JUST KEEP FALLING

CHRISSIE

I watch from the front door of Gaston's condo as he slips on his jacket while he tells my brother and Sam good night. They're sitting on the couch in the living room, each holding a beer. Dinner with him, Mom, Chris, and Sam went great. Mom was her new happy self, and Chris and Sam were both visibly relieved to see just how content she was. Mom spent most of dinner talking about the places the cruise ship was stopping and asking questions about Anna, whom I officially hired after she spent the day working with me.

Then the night got better when, during dessert, my brother and Sam told Mom about their plans to get married and adopt. Mom, like me, couldn't hold back her excitement at hearing the good news and got up, leaving behind her chocolate molten cake to give both guys a hug and to demand through her tears that she get to be there for the wedding, even if it was at a courthouse.

With laughter, they both agreed, and after that, she sat down and called the waiter over to order a bottle of champagne. Being the light-weight she is, she got drunk off two glasses, so after Gus argued with my brother about the bill, won, and paid it, he and I drove Mom home while Sam and Chris followed in her car.

When we arrived at her place, we all walked Mom—who had sobered on the ride—inside, and she decided it was time to pull out the photo albums and show Gus embarrassing pictures of me. We all had a good laugh as she walked him through my childhood, and although I held my breath whenever she came across a photo of my dad, I was impressed she didn't even flinch, even though I did every single time.

Gus, being Gus, noticed the first time it happened and pulled me onto his lap, where he would kiss my shoulder or give my waist a comforting squeeze anytime it happened again. By the time Mom got to my high school album, she was yawning, so once she finished showing Gus my worst two phases—those being me as a hippie and a goth—we left her to go to bed so she could catch her flight in the morning.

When we got back to our building with my brother and Sam, Gus told them he had to get ready to leave for work, so they decided to come up to his place with us so they could hang with me for a while after he left.

Now I'm standing next to the door, hating that he's leaving, even after I've spent the last several hours with him.

"Are you going to be okay sleeping here without me tonight?"

At Gaston's question, I jump and tip my head back toward him, shaking off my wayward thoughts. "I should be," I say, and his expression softens as he pulls me against him, then lowers his face toward mine.

"Call me before you run off into the night with LeFou. I'll have my phone on."

"You mean text," I correct, resting my hands against his chest.

"No." He gives me a squeeze. "I mean use your cell phone's full potential and actually call me if you're scared."

"Fine." I pretend to sound put out. "I'll call you before I run away with your dog."

"Thank you." He smiles.

As I study his smile, I lean into him, then tell him softly, "Thank you for being so awesome. Tonight was perfect."

"You're welcome, sweetheart." He brushes his lips gently over mine, then leans back to look into my eyes while tightening his hold on me. "I'll see you in the morning."

"You'll see me in the morning," I agree, right before he covers my mouth with his and kisses me deeply. When he pulls away, I force myself to let him go, even though I don't want him to leave. And then I give him a small wave as he steps out of his apartment, and I shut the door.

Hearing scratching, I look down and find LeFou pawing at the door. I bend to pick him up, and once I have him against my chest, he licks my jaw. "He'll be back," I say, turning toward the living room, and my steps falter when I find both Chris and Sam smiling at me. "What?" I narrow my eyes on the two of them.

"Nothing." My brother grins. "We're just happy for you."

"Really happy for you," Sam confirms.

Feeling content warmth filling my veins, I walk to the couch and take a seat with LeFou, and Chris comes over to sit next to me.

"He's good for you," my brother says, wrapping his arm around my shoulders as Sam gets up to look around. "I don't think I've ever seen you so content or relaxed."

"That's not surprising, since I've never felt like I do when I'm with him," I tell him honestly.

"That's love." His expression softens in understanding, and I rest my head against his shoulder, thinking he's right.

"Seriously, this place is amazing," Sam says a few minutes later, coming back toward the couch. "I mean, it needs some color, but I'm sure when you move in here you'll fix that."

My stomach drops at his words, but I don't have time to process the thoughts suddenly filling my mind, because Chris's phone dings with a text, and the moment he pulls it out to look at the screen, his body goes rock solid.

"What is it?" I ask him, and he tips his head down toward mine.

"Dad says he'll meet us at two tomorrow afternoon at the diner we used to go to with him and Mom."

My heart sinks, and fear makes my muscles bunch. "Tomorrow is New Year's Eve," I say, not wanting this happy bubble we've built around us to be broken yet.

"I know, but Sam and I won't be around after New Year's, so this is the only time we have to talk to him together. And since there is no way in hell Gaston will be okay with you meeting up with Dad on your own, tomorrow is the only day we have."

Crap, he's right. Even though Gaston has urged me to talk to my dad, if I ever did meet up with him, Gaston would demand to be there with me.

"It will be okay," Chris says, and I want to believe him, but I don't. This last year has proven that the man who raised me, the man whom I called Dad, is no longer a man I know or a guy I like very much. My father was a man of integrity, a man of his word, and a man who loved his family and always put them first.

"You're not doing this on your own, kid," Sam says, coming over to the couch and resting his head over the top of my head. "Your brother, Gus, and I will be there, so even if it's not okay, it will be okay. We'll all make sure of that."

I look up at him, and my mind starts to spin at the idea of him and Gus coming with Chris and me to talk with our dad and all the things that could happen. "I don't think you or Gus should be there," I say, then quickly add, "I mean, I think it would be better if it were just Chris and me, at least at first. Maybe you guys can come in after we've had a chance to talk."

"Are you worried about me or Gus going apeshit?" Sam asks with a smile.

Having known Sam for years, I know that unlike my brother, he is always pretty even tempered. Even in stressful situations, he's never flown off the handle or lashed out in anger. I cannot say the same about Gaston. Even if I've never seen him angry, I know he's protective, and I have no doubt he'd lose his mind if my dad said something he didn't like.

"Gus," I confess, and he doesn't look offended. If anything, he looks pleased with my response.

I feel my brother take hold of my hand, and my eyes go to him. "I think what Sam means is we will all be here after everything is said and done." His fingers squeeze mine. "You're not going through this alone, sis."

At his statement, tears begin to sting the backs of my eyes, and I try to fight them off but know I fail when I feel wetness track down my cheek. Until Gaston came into my life, I didn't think about anything but work. I've spent the last year focused on my shop, so I haven't had to deal with how alone and abandoned I've felt since our father walked out of our lives. Something that was easy to do with Chris living so far away and our mom checking out until recently.

"Please make her stop crying," Sam begs, and I choke on a laughter-filled sob as my brother pulls me into his arms and pats my back, I'm sure glaring at his husband-to-be.

Not wanting either of them to be upset that I'm crying, I quickly pull myself together, then lean back to smile at Sam while wiping my face. "You do know babies cry all the time, right?"

"Yeah. And I've come to terms with our kid being a hellion who's used to always getting their way," he says with a straight face, and I giggle.

"And you're going along with this plan?" I ask Chris.

"We obviously have a difference of opinion," he says, giving me a squeeze before he gets up off the couch and holds out his hand. "All right, show me around this place."

With a deep breath, I let him pull me up; then I show him and Sam around Gaston's condo. My brother agrees halfway through the tour that the place is beautiful, but like Sam said, it needs more color, an observation that makes me smile and feel anxious excitement. Not long after I'm done showing them around, Chris and Sam share a look that I ignore, because *gross*.

I walk them to the door, give them both hugs good night, and tell them I will see them in the morning for breakfast with Gaston. When they leave, I let LeFou outside on the balcony to potty one last time. I lock up after I let him back in, then go to the bedroom, change into my nightgown, and take off my makeup. I crawl into bed and call Gaston so I can tell him about my impending meeting with my dad, and not surprisingly, he tells me he's going with me, even if he'll just be sitting outside the restaurant with Sam.

By the time I hang up with him, I'm feeling a little less anxious about tomorrow, and I'm so tired I don't have a chance to be scared. I fall asleep as soon as I get off the phone, and when I wake up again, Gaston is pulling me against his warm body. I absently feel him kiss my forehead, and then I fall back asleep, feeling nothing but contentment in his arms.

"Me and Sam will be here when you two come out," Gus tells me before capturing me behind my neck with his hand and pulling me forward against his warm, strong body. My arms automatically circle his waist, and I settle against him, wishing he were coming into the restaurant with me. "If anything is said that you don't like, or if you feel the slightest bit uncomfortable, get up and walk out," he says quietly, and I rest my forehead against his chest, feeling his lips rest heavy against my hair. I take a few deep breaths, summoning the courage I need, and then pull my forehead away from where it's resting and tip my head back toward him, accepting a soft kiss. "Don't forget what I said."

"I won't," I whisper as I feel a hand touch my lower back. I turn to look at my brother, who seems way more prepared for this than I am.

"Ready?" Chris asks.

"Yeah." I give him a jerky nod, and Gus lets me go so I can take Chris's hand when he reaches it out toward me.

With my knees feeling weak, I walk hand in hand with my brother into the diner where we're meeting our dad, and as soon as we walk through the door, I spot him. He looks different from the last time, older even, sitting alone in a booth with his head bent over his hands, which are curled around a cup of coffee in front of him.

I absently hear Chris tell a waitress that we're meeting someone but won't be staying long as my dad lifts his head, and my stomach rolls when I catch a glimpse of pain shoot through his features. "Come on," Chris says, and before I can prepare, he gives my hand, still held firmly in his, a tug, then proceeds to pull me with him across the restaurant to the booth our father is seated at.

Dad gets up to stand at the side of the table as we walk toward him, and I fight against the urge to either run and greet him like I always did when I was younger, or run away, back to the safety of Gaston outside.

"Dad," Chris says, giving my hand a reassuring squeeze before letting me go to slide into the booth.

I hesitate, wringing my hands together, not sure I'm ready to do this. Actually, I'm sure I'm not. I feel eyes on me, and I glance at my brother, who's studying our father, and then my eyes move automatically to him.

"Please sit, honey," my dad pleads, looking worried as he takes a seat.

With my stomach turning, I slide across the red pleather seat, getting as close to my brother as I possibly can, and Chris lifts his arm, then wraps it around my shoulders. I lean into him as an uncomfortable silence settles over the table, and I hold my breath, waiting for someone to speak, knowing it's not going to be me who breaks the silence.

"You both look well," Dad finally says, and I feel Chris shift as the muscles in his waist and arm tighten. "How have you two been?"

"Seriously?" Chris bites out. "Over a year, and the first words out of your mouth are 'You look well' and 'How have you been?'"

"Son," Dad murmurs, and Chris's body gets so tight against mine that I have to wiggle out of his hold, afraid he'll accidentally strangle me.

"Son?" Chris hisses, leaning across the table toward Dad, who now looks pale. "Are you fucking joking? I haven't spoken to you since you told Mom you wanted a divorce. I don't know you." Chris points his finger at Dad's pale face. "You're not my dad. You're not the man who raised me. The man I knew as my father was honest, and he loved his family. I don't know who you are."

"I'm sorry," Dad whispers. Even as angry as I am with him, I still hate the pain I see in his features as he looks between Chris and me. "I'm sorry."

My eyes slide closed, and tears start to build behind my eyelids. "Give us something," I whisper before pulling in a deep breath. When I open my eyes, I look at my father, the first man I ever loved, and beg, "Please, make us understand what happened."

"I don't . . ." He visibly swallows. "I don't have an excuse. I wish I did, but I don't."

"Chrissie and I are both grown. We understand people fall out of love; we get that relationships end," Chris states, and I hear him pull in an audible breath before he continues. "What we don't understand is you cutting us out of your life."

"I didn't want to hurt either of you, and I thought if I . . ." He jerks his head from side to side. "I didn't think either of you would want anything to do with me after I left your mom."

"Shouldn't that have been our decision?" I ask, and he reaches for my hands on the table between us. I pull them away before he can grasp them and lean back, clasping them in my lap and shaking my head. "You should have spoken to us. You should have given us the opportunity to hear you out and decide on our own how to move forward. You didn't do that."

"I don't know what you want me to say," he insists after a moment, sounding frustrated.

Anger fills the pit of my stomach at his tone, and I lean forward. "I don't know about Chris, but I want you to admit you messed up." Tears fill my eyes, which are locked with his. "I want you to tell me you're sorry for not reaching out since you and Mom split up, and I want you to show that you understand how deeply you hurt me when you didn't even call to make sure I was okay after I saw you with the woman you left Mom for."

"Tammy," he inserts.

My head jerks back in confusion. "What?"

"My wife's name is Tammy."

"Your wife. The woman you cheated on our mother with for God knows how long doesn't factor into this situation," Chris hisses, and Dad leans back with his jaw ticking. "What you're not getting is that she means nothing to us, because you didn't want her to. After you left Mom, you didn't introduce us to her. And you sure as fuck have never given us the opportunity to get to know her. She is just the woman you married after you left our mother, the woman who knew you had a family but was okay with carrying on a relationship with you for however long before you decided to end things with your wife and marry *her* instead."

"She wasn't happy with the way things happened between us. And she wanted to meet you—wants to meet you," Dad says quietly, holding my brother's eyes.

"Yeah," Chris begins, and I turn to see that his jaw's so tight it's clenching. "You wanna know the most fucked-up thing about this whole situation?" he asks, but he doesn't give Dad a chance to answer. "If you had gone about things differently, I'd want to meet her too. I'd want to get to know her and see you two together." He jerks his head from side to side.

"Chris," Dad starts, but Chris shakes his head again.

"No, that's the most fucked-up part about this whole situation. You have been so self-consumed that you've let the people who love you the most down, because you haven't trusted them to love you in spite of your actions."

"I want you and your sister to meet Tammy," Dad states, and even though I'm not looking at him, I feel his eyes on me. "I miss you both."

"Could've fooled me, considering you ran into your daughter with your new wife, saw she was visibly upset, and didn't even call her after to make sure she was okay."

"I didn't think you'd want to hear from me," Dad explained, and I look across the table to meet his sorrowful gaze. "I'm sorry. I wanted to call you; I just didn't think you'd want me to."

"You should have called," I tell him, and he drops his eyes from mine. "I hate this," I whisper after a moment, and his head lifts. "I hate that I miss you, hate what has happened, and really hate that you didn't trust us to still love you, even if you weren't in love with Mom."

"How do I fix this?" he asks, and my heart hurts, because I honestly don't know if there is a way to fix this. So much has happened over the last year, and I don't know if I can forgive him for everything he's done.

"I don't know," I tell him, and his eyes start to fill with tears.

"Dad," Chris calls, and Dad's eyes go to him, and so do mine. "You might not ever fix what you've done, but I do know that if you don't try, you never will. It's going to take time for Chrissie and me to trust you again, and the only way you're going to rebuild that trust is by showing up and putting in the work. You let both of us down."

"I know. Believe me, I know, because I let myself down too," Dad says, looking defeated, and his pain-filled words slice through my heart. "I promise, if you two give me a chance, I'll do what I have to do to fix this."

"Just be my dad again," I plead, and he looks at me. "All I've wanted from you over the last year is for you to be my dad." I pull in a shaky breath. "I've missed you."

"I miss you too, honey," he tells me, looking at me, and then his eyes go to Chris. "I miss you too, son."

"Then prove it, because I'd like you around," Chris says, his voice sounding rough. "Chrissie and I will both at some point get married and start our own families. I'd like my kids to know all of their grand-parents, and I'm sure Chrissie feels the same about that."

I reach under the table and take my brother's hand, giving it a comforting squeeze. His anger at my dad might be winning out right now, but there is no doubt after hearing his words or the tone in which he spoke that he's been hurting just as badly as I have.

"I'll prove it," Dad agrees, sounding choked up, and then he glances around. "Do you two want to have lunch with me?"

Chris lifts his chin, then dips his head down toward me, and I tell him without words that I don't want that—not yet anyway. "Sorry, we have stuff going on tonight that we have to get ready for," he tells Dad.

"Right, sorry. It's New Year's Eve. I didn't think."

"Sam and I leave to head home the day after tomorrow. I know Chrissie has to work, but if you want, maybe Sam and I can meet you for lunch tomorrow afternoon?"

"I'd really like that. Tell me the time and the place, and I'll be there," Dad says immediately, and then he looks at me. "If you let me know when you have time, I'd like to get together with you, even if it's just to have coffee."

"Call, and we will figure something out," I agree, and his expression fills with determination.

"I'll call," he tells me, and then he looks out the window for a moment before looking back between Chris and me. "I'm glad you're both braver than me. Thank you for reaching out."

I swallow, having nothing to say, and Chris's fingers convulse around mine. "We should go," he says, urging me out of the booth, and I stand while our dad does the same. Once we're all up, Dad gives me a hug, and I fight to hold back tears and then let him go so he can embrace Chris. When my brother steps away, he takes my hand once more. "We'll talk soon."

"We will," Dad confirms, and then his gaze comes to me, communicating the same statement. "Have a good New Year's," he says, and then he sits back in the booth, and we walk out of the restaurant. I turn to look over my shoulder before the door closes and watch Dad's new wife come from wherever she'd been sitting and wrap her arms around him as his shoulders shake. Seeing that, I feel a little better, and then I feel a whole lot better when I find Gaston waiting for me with a worried look and his arms open wide.

"You okay?" he asks, enveloping me in a hug, and I nod against his chest, thinking that yes, finally, I really am okay. Maybe, just maybe, I'll get a relationship back with my father, and even if that doesn't happen, I have the love of a really great man to help me deal with that pain.

Suggestion 16

Do Not Freak Out

CHRISSIE

I look over my shoulder when I hear keys in the lock, and I hold my breath when the door opens and Gaston walks in carrying a large suitcase, followed by his mom. She looks about my height as she's standing at his side, with a slim build, his same dark hair, and gorgeous eyes. I stand from the couch and start to wring my hands together. Gaston's gaze drops to my hands, and he grins like he thinks the nervous gesture is cute.

I wanted to go with him to the airport when he left to pick up his mom, but I also wanted to give him and his mom a little time alone, and I didn't feel right leaving Sam and Chris here. Which ended up being pointless, because they both left not long after Gus did, claiming they wanted to go take a nap. I find his mom studying me with an open curiosity that causes my nervousness to increase. I don't remember ever meeting any of my previous boyfriends' parents before, and even if I had, it wouldn't have meant anything. Gaston's the first guy I've been in love with, the first guy where meeting his mom actually means something.

"Sweetheart, are you going to just stand there, or are you going to come over here so I can introduce you to my mom?"

His mom laughs, and my cheeks get pink with embarrassment as I walk toward them. Once I'm close, he reaches out for me.

I settle against his side, then look at his mom, smile awkwardly, and say, "Hi."

"You were right. She's beautiful," she tells him while taking my hand, and my heart swells.

"Chrissie, my mom, Rita. Mom . . . Chrissie." Gaston lets me go when Rita gives my hand a gentle tug, and then she startles me by reaching up to touch my face.

"My son has been telling me about you since the first night he met you, and I have to admit I've enjoyed the stories, but my favorite is the one of you two meeting and you telling him to leave you alone."

"You told her I said that?" I look at Gaston, and I'm sure I look horrified.

"It was cute." He smiles, and I shake my head.

"I didn't actually mean he should leave me alone. It was just . . . he looks like him and is all . . ." My cheeks get hotter. "I'm sure you know, since you raised him, and I couldn't think straight when he was around me."

She laughs and Gaston does too, while I wish the ground would open and swallow me whole. "He does seem to make women a little scatterbrained." She touches the side of her head, and I can't hold back the giggle that escapes.

"Believe me, I know. I now have three girls who work for me, and anytime he comes into my shop, none of them seem to know up from down."

"He drove me by your bakery on the way here." Her smile is soft. "It's very cute. I hope you can give me a tour while I'm in town."

"I would love that," I say, thinking this is much easier than I thought it would be. I truly thought Gaston was lying about how easygoing his mom was, and how excited she was to meet me, just so I would feel better about staying with him while she was in town.

"We will make it happen," she states, and then she glances around. "Gaston mentioned your brother and his fiancé are here."

"They are. They left not long ago to go take a nap, since tonight is going to be a late one."

"I think I might do the same," she says, giving my hand she's still holding a squeeze. "It really is nice to finally meet you, and I'm looking forward to getting to know you while I'm in town."

"Me too," I reply, and she smiles, letting my hand go before looking up at her son.

"Am I staying in the same room as last time?"

"Yeah," he says.

"All right, I'll see you this evening, Chrissie."

"See you later," I say to her back when she turns to walk toward the two spare rooms located down the hall.

"That wasn't so bad, was it?" Gaston asks, and I shake my head. "Told you so." I roll my eyes at the smug look on his face, and he laughs, then leans in to kiss my forehead. "I'm going to get her settled. I'll be back."

"I'll be here," I reply, and he smiles, lifting his fingers to touch the side of my face before carrying his mom's suitcase away. I take a seat on the couch and pick up my phone to call Leah and tell her what happened today, and to make sure we're still set for tonight. But I pause when I see a text waiting for me on the screen from my dad.

Thank you for meeting with me today. I love you, honey.

I stare at the message, feeling a million different things, the biggest of them all being hope. With a few quick swipes, I text him back with a simple I love you too, and I tell him I hope we can meet for coffee this week. After I press send, I dial Leah, whom I just spoke to a few days ago, but with everything that's happened and everything I have to tell her, you'd think we haven't spoken in a year. When I get off the phone after talking with her, I find Gaston in the kitchen.

"Is your mom okay?"

"Yep, settled in and going to take a nap." His eyes come to me. "Do turkey sandwiches for lunch sound okay?"

"Sure, do you want me to help?"

"I got it. Just grab chips and drinks, baby," he says, then asks, "Was that Leah on the phone?"

"Yeah, I wanted to call to make sure she and Tyler are still planning to meet us at the restaurant, and to tell her about meeting up with my dad this morning."

"What'd she say about that?"

"She's glad I finally talked to him," I reply, grabbing a bag of chips from the pantry and two Cokes from the fridge while he smears mayo on four pieces of dark bread, then piles them high with turkey and swiss cheese. I go to the fridge and grab a jar of sweet dill pickles and hand it to him, making him smile. "Also, my dad sent me a text." His gaze comes to me. "Hopefully, that means today actually did get through to him."

"Only time will tell, sweetheart." He cuts both sandwiches in half, then places each on a plate. "Let's eat in the bedroom."

"Is that code for something else?" I wink, grabbing the chips and drinks and listening to him as he laughs.

"I wish. Unfortunately, I only have time to eat lunch with you," he says as I get onto his bed. He hands me a plate before sitting next to me. "I have to go to Twilight to take care of a few last-minute things."

I take a bite of my sandwich and groan in approval. Once I've chewed and swallowed, I ask, "Is there anything I can help you with?"

"No, everything is covered." He leans over to give me a kiss, then reaches for his Coke. He takes a sip, and I notice he's already half-finished with his sandwich, making my heart sink, because that means he will be leaving me soon.

"I really hate that you have to leave."

At my statement, his eyes come to me, and whatever he sees in my expression makes his face soften. "Sorry, baby." He drops his plate to his side table, then removes mine from my lap and places his face close to mine. "I can't wait until this shit is over."

"The holidays?" I ask, and he shakes his head, searching my gaze.

"No, the leaving you in bed all the time."

"Me too," I agree; then his mouth covers mine, and a simple kiss turns into a make-out session and a really quick quickie before he leaves me in bed, our half-eaten sandwiches forgotten as he goes to get ready for work.

When he comes out dressed, I'm lying on my stomach dozing, and he kisses my bare shoulder, making me smile. "Thanks for the sandwich and the orgasm," I say.

He chuckles, kissing my temple, and then orders, "Sleep, and I'll be back to wake you with plenty of time for you to get ready for dinner."

"Okay," I agree, already half-asleep, with my eyes drooping closed.

"Love you," I hear, and then I listen to the rattle of plates, the door closing, and LeFou jumping up onto the bed as he curls against my side. I pass out two seconds later, and I do it with a smile on my face.

Standing on a small platform above the crowded club, I smile when I hear Leah giggle. "She's good," she says, referring to Gaston's mom, who is currently flirting with one of the young, very attractive male waiters, Allen, who's been taking care of us since we got here.

"She really is." I watch the waiter lean in to whisper something in her ear, and I wonder how Gaston would feel if he were to see what was happening right now between his mom and one of his employees.

"I think she and Gram might have been separated at birth," Leah says, referring to her grandmother, whose love life is still very, very active.

I laugh so hard tears fill my eyes and then look at my best friend. "I think we should ask them to do a DNA test."

"Right." She grins as she studies me, and then her hand wraps around mine, and her face sobers. "I know I said this earlier, while we were at the restaurant, but I want to say it again. I'm happy for you. Gaston is awesome and so very perfect for you."

"Thank you," I say through the tightness in my throat as she pulls me in for a hug.

I hug her back tightly, rocking her back and forth. I feel someone nearby, so I let her go and find one of the other VIP waitresses, Samantha, a beautiful woman with long black hair, holding a tray with a single glass of champagne. "This is for you," she tells me, and I wonder who sent the glass. All evening, she and our waiter have been bringing glasses of alcohol to each of us randomly on the VIP platform from people partying on the club floor.

"Thank you. That's sweet, but I'm cutting myself off until I get home," I tell her, leaving out that I already had two glasses of wine at dinner and a glass since I've been here. I know if I drink any more, I will be snoozing on the couch Sam and Chris are currently sitting on. She nods like she understands, and not a second later, Gaston's mom walks up and takes the glass, smiling.

"She's cut herself off, but I haven't done the same." She tips the glass back and swallows half of it in one gulp before finishing it and placing the empty glass back on Samantha's tray.

I laugh when she grins, and then I look down when she holds out her hand toward me. "Let's dance."

"Um . . ." I look to Leah for help, and she smiles at me right before she gasps, because Rita grabs her hand along with mine, then drags us off the VIP platform and down into the crowd of people dancing to the music the live DJ is playing. With no other choice, I dance with Gaston's mom, whom I'm falling in love with, and my best friend for a few songs.

I feel eyes on me when the music starts to change to something I'm not even sure how to move to, and I look up to the platform and find Gaston watching me with a look of amused frustration and Tyler looking at his wife with the same expression on his handsome face. I know their look has to do with the group of men who have been attempting to get us to dance with them for the last few minutes. I get Leah's attention, then point in the guys' direction, and she giggles before grabbing Rita's hand and urging her to follow us. Once we reach the VIP platform, the scary-looking security guard standing at the bottom of the steps lifts the red rope, letting us through.

I take the bottle that my brother, who is standing next to Sam, holds out to me, and I notice both of them looking highly amused as they glance at Gaston. I roll my eyes at them as I twist off the top of the water bottle and take a sip.

"Are you having fun?" Gaston whispers into my ear, and I look at him over my shoulder as his arms circle my waist.

"Yes." I smile, turning in his arms, and I rest my hands, including the one still grasping the bottle, against his chest as I see his mom smile at us. "I love your mom. She's awesome."

"It's good you think that, since she feels the same," he says, taking the bottle from me and passing it to Chris.

"You think so?" I ask, and he grins.

"The moment she got me alone this afternoon after her nap, she was on my ass about my intentions, sweetheart."

"What?" I breathe, pressing myself impossibly closer to him.

He smiles, tucking some of my hair behind my ear. "My mom might not have wanted to get married or be tied down, but that doesn't mean she wants the same for me." He leans closer, so close I feel his breath whisper across my lips as he speaks. "She's been champing at the bit for grandkids since I moved out on my own. She's kept that under wraps, but after spending the afternoon with you, she's been asking when we're going to give her little ones to spoil."

"Oh," I whisper, having nothing else to say, because seriously, there is nothing to say. I know I'm in love with him, but marriage and babies at this point might be more than I can handle. I already feel like we're moving at the speed of sound; a baby would push us past that, toward light speed.

"Don't worry. I tucked your birth control somewhere she will never look so she won't hide it from you." He laughs, reading my look, and I giggle, dropping my forehead to rest against his chin. His hand moves to my jaw, and his thumb skims across my lower lip as he tips my head back to meet his warm gaze. "I love you."

"I love you too," I whisper before he lowers his head to place his lips against mine. I accept his kiss, then smile against his mouth and giggle when I hear Leah shout a loud "I told you so!"

"Your friend is as crazy as you are," he tells me. I look around at Leah, who's giving me a thumbs-up from where she's tucked against Tyler's side.

"She's crazier than me," I say, and Gaston shakes his head.

"Your crazy might be silent and hers might be vocalized, but you're both insane."

"Whatever." I laugh, and his eyes bore into mine before he drops his head to kiss me again, this time longer than before. When he pulls away, I'm half-drunk on his kiss.

"I hate to say this, baby, but you guys should go before traffic gets so bad you spend New Year's Eve watching the fireworks from your car."

"Aren't you coming with us?" I ask, and he shakes his head, causing disappointment to fill my stomach.

"I need to stay at least a couple more hours, but I'll be there to ring in the New Year with you."

"You just admitted traffic is going to be crazy, so unless you plan on arriving in your spaceship, how are you going to make that happen?"

"I have my bike. It's parked out back, so even if there's traffic, I'll make my way through it and be there to kiss you at midnight."

I tip my head to the side while lifting my hands to each side of his face, and then I tell him quietly, "You know I love you. You don't have to keep your true identity from me. I won't tell the government about you."

He tosses his head back to laugh; then, still laughing, he places his lips over mine. I soak up the feeling of his kiss and his happiness before he pulls away.

"It's good to know you have my back, sweetheart." His voice is filled with humor as he turns me into his side and leads me to our families and friends. Once he's passed me off to my brother with instructions to get me home safe, he looks at his mom, and I do the same, noticing she looks a little pale. "Are you okay, Mom?" he asks her.

"I think I've drunk too much wine. I'll be okay," she tells him with a wave of her hand.

"Are you sure, Rita?" I take a few steps closer to her and place my hand on her arm, not liking the color of her skin or the way her eyes seem to take longer than normal to focus on me.

"I'm sure," she says, wobbling, and my heart drops into the pit of my stomach as she suddenly reaches out for me, grabbing hold of the top of my dress and ripping it as she falls. With a startled cry, I try to catch her, but her weight is more than I can bear alone, and I hit the ground with her landing half on top of me. Commotion surrounds us as everyone jumps into action, lifting her then me off the ground. I stare horrified at Rita as she's placed on a couch, and I hold my breath when Gaston shouts in a fear-filled voice for someone to call an ambulance as he drops to his knees and begins to check his mom.

"Are you okay?" Leah asks me worriedly, holding my arm as I grasp the top of my dress with my hands.

"I'm fine," I tell her shakily before I rush to Gaston's side, dropping to my knees next to him. "Is she okay?"

"I don't know," he says, and I lean in closer, then reach out for her hand, wrapping my fingers around her wrist to check her pulse. When I was working as a manager at the restaurant, the owner required us all to take CPR classes just in case someone ever choked. Thankfully, our instructors were thorough in everything they taught us.

"Her pulse and breathing are both normal," I tell Gus when I feel the steady beat of his mom's pulse against the tips of my fingers, and I watch her chest rise and fall without wavering.

"That might be, but something isn't right," he tells me as he lifts her head to the side and it falls right back against her shoulder without him holding it up.

"An ambulance is on the way." I know it's Tyler speaking. I look over my shoulder and find him holding his phone to his ear, with Leah, who looks completely freaked, tucked under his arm. "They say they're less than five minutes away."

"Thanks," I whisper to him, and then I turn my attention back to Rita, who hasn't moved, even with her son calling her name and trying to get her to respond.

It feels like it takes a lot longer than five minutes for the paramedics to show up; then when they do, it's a whirlwind of activity. They quickly check to make sure she is stable, and once they see she is, they load her onto a stretcher, and with Gaston right at her side and me close behind, we leave the club and go with them to the ambulance parked outside at the curb.

"Who's riding with her?" one of the paramedics asks, looking at the group of people who've come outside.

"I am," Gaston says, and then he looks through the crowd that seems to be closing in around us. When his eyes land on me, I can tell he's torn.

"I'll meet you at the hospital," I tell him softly, and with a jerk of his chin and a look at Chris, he gets into the back of the ambulance with the paramedics to ride with his mom.

"We'll drive you." A warm hand lands on my shoulder, and I turn to find Tyler and Leah.

"Thank you," I whisper as my brother wraps his arm around me, with Sam close to my side and Leah looking back at me every few seconds.

When we get to the hospital, Tyler and Chris find out from a nurse that Rita has been placed in a room and that we have to wait in the waiting area for someone to come out and talk to us.

Not sure what is happening with Gaston or his mom, I pace back and forth across the tile floors, jumping every single time the doors at the end of the hall open up until I eventually give in to the urge to cry. Sam pulls me down to sit next to him. With my face tucked against his chest and my tears dried up, I lift my head when I hear the swoosh of the automatic doors. I don't expect to see Gaston, but when I do, I let out the breath that has been trapped in my lungs since I watched him get into the back of the ambulance with his mom.

I stand quickly, then rush to him, feeling his hands curve around my waist as mine land on his chest. "Is she okay?"

"She's fine." His jaw tics. "She's a little out of it, but she's awake, and the doctor told me she will be okay."

I sag against him in relief and then ask, "What happened?"

"She was drugged," he says.

I gasp as my head jerks back. "What?"

"They ran a few tests and found that she had Rohypnol in her system."

"Oh my God." I cover my mouth and stare at him in horror.

"Mom said the last thing she really remembers is taking a drink that was brought up to you in the VIP."

"To me?" I ask, confused. All night, drinks were brought to the VIP section to each and every one of us. More than once, I turned a drink away because I didn't want to get drunk. "Are you telling me that drink was meant for me?"

"Sweetheart." Gaston captures me around the waist as I attempt to pull away from him.

"I cannot believe this."

"Security at the club has already gone over the footage from the time you entered the club to when the paramedics showed up," he says, and I notice his jaw is clenching in anger. "I know who laced the drink, and the police have already been notified and are probably already arresting her."

"Who? Why would someone do something like that?" I ask, and his eyes close. I grab hold of his biceps and squeeze until his focus is on me.

"It was Georgia," he finally answers, and I stare at him.

"Georgia? Your bar manager?"

"Yes," he says, sounding angry. "She . . . fuck! I thought we talked shit out and that she was over whatever shit she had in her head." I can tell he's not even talking to me; he's just talking, and I want to shake him.

"She had a thing for you?" It's a statement, not a question, and he nods.

"I don't even know what to say," I admit, wrapping my arms around him.

"Me neither," he says, and I feel his breath at the top of my head.

"I'm glad your mom is okay."

"Yeah, me too," he murmurs, holding me close, and my eyes slide closed. I soak in the feeling of being in his arms and the warmth of knowing his mom is okay, and I pray that Georgia, whoever she is, gets what she deserves.

Suggestion 17

REMEMBER: THIS IS FOREVER

GASTON

"I'm home," I call out, shutting the door behind me, and then I drop my keys into the bowl on the table near the door and shout, "Chrissie!" When I don't hear her shout back from wherever she is, I walk down the two steps into the sunken living room, no longer really noticing the colorful art on the walls, the bright pillows and throws tossed on the couch, or the photos and what Chrissie calls "knickknacks" littering every surface.

She officially moved in six months ago, about a month and a half after Georgia tried to drug her and instead drugged my mom. I found out she told one of the waitresses that her plan was to drug Chrissie, place her in a compromising position with a guy, and get photos that she would later show me. In her mind, I would see the evidence of Chrissie cheating on me and turn to her for comfort. The waitress thought Georgia was joking when she told her the plan, so she didn't come to me and tell me, which she regretted after she saw my mom being loaded onto a stretcher.

I also found out Georgia was the one behind the missing alcohol. When the police went to her apartment to search for evidence, they found bottles on top of bottles of liquor. Knowing I owned a club and two bars, they looked into things and realized she had stolen the alcohol from the club and was selling it on the side at half the price—something she had apparently been doing for a while but had never gotten caught, because she never took more than a bottle at a time.

That is, she didn't until the order I placed before New Year's. She got greedy then and thought she would be able to make a huge chunk of change if she could get rid of it. She didn't consider that most people don't drink top-shelf alcohol, and almost no one is willing to spend a few hundred dollars on alcohol they aren't even sure is legit.

I shake off those thoughts and look around. With LeFou and Chrissie not being in the kitchen or living room, I stop at the balcony doors to look out and see if they are sitting outside, where I sometimes find Chrissie in the mornings or evenings curled up with a book or a glass of wine.

Not seeing her there but knowing she's home, because her car was parked in the spot next to mine, I walk back by the kitchen and across the living room to the bedroom at the end of a short hallway. A hallway that is now lined with photos of us, our friends, and our families. I reach the bedroom and open the door, finding the room empty. My gut tightens as I look around until I hear the bathtub jets going and notice the door to the bathroom is closed. With an altogether different kind of tightness in my gut, I pull my shirt off over my head and walk across the room.

As soon as I enter the dimly lit room, I know something is up. Chrissie is in the tub, and like normal when she has the jets going, LeFou is at the side making sure she's okay. I get close, and when I do, her eyes pop open and her startled gaze meets mine. That's when I notice she's been crying.

"You're home."

"You're crying." I feel my heart twist at the sight of her wet cheeks, and my mind races as I try to think of what could have her upset, but nothing at all comes to mind. For the last six months, everything in our lives has been good. Better than good. Anna, Chrissie's new shop manager, has settled right into her role without any kind of issues, and Chrissie has been able to take time off each week.

Chrissie has also been rebuilding a relationship with her dad, who's made it a point to call or show up at her shop just to spend time with her, and she and I even had dinner with him and his wife, Tammy. Her mom is still happy; she started dating and has been traveling a lot. Her brother and Sam got married four months ago, and two months after they said "I do" they got a call in the middle of the night from their adoption caseworker telling them that a baby had been abandoned at their local hospital. She explained that the child's mother was a drug user, which meant they would have to be open to taking care of a drug-addicted newborn who might not make it. They didn't even think about it; they went to the hospital that night and quickly fell in love with their daughter. At first things didn't look good, but the little girl they named Destiny fought while we all prayed, and after six weeks they were able to take her home. Just last week we flew up to spend a few days with them, and just like they had, Chrissie and I fell in love with her on sight. My mom is still my mom—wild, crazy, and always on some adventure but healthy and living her best life. My sisters are both doing great. Just a few months ago, Chrissie and I flew down to Florida so she could meet them, along with my stepmom. It was a great trip, and it was nice to be able to share a piece of my dad with Chrissie, even if he wasn't there.

Then there's Chrissie and me. We are still falling in love, and every day I learn something new about her that makes me love her even more, which seems impossible.

"No, I'm not." Her whispered words pull me from my thoughts, and I watch her wipe her cheeks.

I ignore her absurd lie and move LeFou out of the way to kneel down next to the tub. "Why are you crying?" I ask, touching her face with the backs of my fingers. I hate her tears.

"I'm not. The jets are going, so the water is splashing on my face, making it look like I am."

"What happened?" I ask, skimming my fingers down the side of her face.

"Nothing."

Knowing how stubborn she can be, I stand up to get undressed so I can get into the tub with her. I start to kick off my shoes when a bag with a small white box inside it catches my attention. I shouldn't even notice it, not with the amount of stuff she has lying out on the counter, but I still do. Without thinking, I pick up the bag and absently hear her say my name as I pull out the opened box to read the front of it.

"Are you pregnant?" I turn around toward her, and she covers her face with her hands and sobs. Not sure what to do in this situation, I set down the box and finish getting undressed. I climb into the tub behind her and wrap my arms around her chest, then place my lips against her ear. "Talk to me, sweetheart."

"My period is late." Her hands wrap around my arm across her chest. "I took a test just to make sure, and I thought for sure it would be negative, since I'm on birth control."

"It wasn't?"

"No." She lowers her head to her chest. "The first test I took told me I was pregnant, so I took another one, and it said the same thing."

With my heart suddenly overfull, I rest the side of my head against hers and pull in a deep breath. "We're having a baby."

"That's what the tests say, but I don't know how that's possible. I haven't missed a pill. Birth control is supposed to be ninety-nine point nine-nine percent effective."

"If you're pregnant, it's obviously meant to be," I tell her, sliding my hand down her wet skin to rest against her stomach. I've never considered being baited and caught by a woman who was completely right for me, so it shouldn't surprise me that something that should happen has happened. "This thing between us was meant to be, and tomorrow, you'll call your doctor to see if the test you took was correct. If it is, I'll be happy, and I know you will too."

"We're not even married," she sobs, and I want to laugh. We might not be married, but two people couldn't be more committed than us.

"We'll get married."

"Why? Because I'm pregnant?" she asks with her voice sounding shaky.

"No, because I love you and I can't imagine spending the rest of my life without you," I tell her, thinking about the engagement ring I bought that's been sitting in my drawer for weeks as I've tried to come up with the perfect way to ask her to marry me.

"We just moved in together. Heck, we just started dating. This is—"

"This is us. Since the beginning, we have done things a little differently."

"You mean fast," she says, and I smile, then kiss her shoulder.

"Everything might be fast, but you can't deny that this is right. From the moment we met, I've wanted more from you—more time, more kisses, more of you falling asleep next to me, more of your laughter, and a lot more of your love. I can't get enough of you. So yes, what's happened has happened fast, but what's happened has been right, from the very beginning."

"A baby," she whispers, and I know she's scared. I get it, because it is scary. Hell, I'm freaking out a little, but I know everything will be okay.

"The moment you hold our son or daughter the first time, I promise you it's going to feel like the exact right moment."

"Leah and Tyler aren't even pregnant," she inserts, and I realize what most of her tears are about. Yes, I'm sure she's afraid, but she loves her best friend and has seen how stressed Leah has been each month when she's gotten a negative test result.

"Sweetheart, if the shoe were on the opposite foot, would you be happy for Leah if she told you she was pregnant?"

"Of course I would be." She gasps, sounding offended that I'd think otherwise, and I fight back laughter.

"She'll be happy for you too. So before you start creating problems where there aren't any, let's just deal with you carrying our child safely for the next nine months, us getting married, and all the other things that will happen before our baby gets here."

"I'm not creating problems."

I don't even bother responding to her statement, since I know it will only encourage her to fight her corner.

"I'm *not* creating problems." She huffs, crossing her arms over her chest, and this time, I do actually laugh. "This isn't funny."

"I know." I kiss her shoulder. "Since you're in a mood to fight, I think you should also know you won't be working as much as you do now."

"Pardon?" She turns her head to glare at me.

"You're carrying our child. You need to rest, and working fifteen-hour days is not good for you, and for sure it's not good for the baby."

"You just . . . I just can't believe you."

"You hired Anna, and I know she's good at her job and that she can handle things in your absence. You need to let her do that."

"I've been taking a day off every week."

"Yeah, but you could take two, cut back your hours, and let her cover things."

"Rachelle and Aubrey are gone," she says, sounding sad.

"Yeah, and since they left, you've been dragging your feet on replacing them."

"Why are you being annoying right now?"

"You only think I'm annoying right now because you know I'm right. You can't only think about you anymore." I touch my hand to her stomach under the water, and her breath catches. "You're pregnant. I know you just found out and that it's going to take you a little time to come to terms with that, but I want you and our baby healthy. So if I have to tie you to the bed for the next nine months to make sure you're taken care of, that's what I will do."

"Why are you so okay with this?" She tips her head down as she places her hand over the top of mine.

"I'm okay with it because I know what a miracle it is and because I already knew I wanted kids with you someday," I say, and she sighs, then leans her head back to rest against my shoulder.

"My mom is going to freak."

"Your mom is going to be thrilled, and so is everyone else."

"You know, it's really frustrating that you're not freaking out, especially since you're the guy and should be the one freaking out right now."

"Is that written in blood somewhere?"

"No, spaceman, it's just normal Earth male behavior," she grumbles, and I chuckle, then kiss the side of her head.

"Are you ready to get out of the bath?"

"Not really, but I'm hungry, so I'm going to have to get up," she says, turning to her stomach, and the moment her soft belly brushes my cock, it comes to life between us.

"Come here." I pull her up my body, and her legs fall open to rest on either side of my hips.

"What?" she asks, resting her hands against my chest, sounding suddenly turned on.

"Do you love me?" I prompt, sliding my hand around the back of her neck.

Her face softens. "Yes."

"And you know I love you, right?"

"Yes," she repeats, searching my eyes.

"I'm here. We're in this together, and I promise everything is going to be okay."

"Okay," she says softly.

"Okay," I reiterate, and then I pull her face down for a kiss and groan when she rolls her hips against mine as the head of my cock bumps her entrance.

"Chrissie," I warn, capturing her hip with one hand.

"Gaston." She smiles against my lips before rolling her hips once more, sliding me deeper.

"Fuck," I hiss as her pussy ripples.

"Yes," she whimpers, taking all of me, and my fingers dig into her flesh as she stills, looking down at me. "I might be scared out of my mind, but one thing I know for certain—there is no one else I'd want to have a baby with, no one else I will ever love the way I love you. So you're right—it's going to take me some time to get used to the idea of becoming a mom, but I know I will get used to it, and I'll do that because I have you."

"Are you going to spend the rest of your life with me?" I ask, and her face softens while her pussy tightens like a vise.

"Yes," she answers, and I drop my hand from behind her neck, then wrap both my palms around her waist.

"Move, baby," I order, feeling overwhelmed with emotion. I can't believe this gorgeous woman is mine, that I get to spend the rest of my life with her, and that she is carrying my child. "You gotta move, sweetheart. Otherwise, I'm going to fuck you, and I can't promise I'll be gentle."

"Then fuck me," she taunts, and I clench my teeth against the urge to fuck her.

"Chrissie."

"You won't hurt me or the baby. So please, fuck me."

At her words, I lift my hips while I pull her down hard, then keep doing it over and over, listening to the sounds of her pleasure bouncing off the walls and the water sloshing out of the tub. When I know she's close, feel the tightness, and see her eyes go half-mast, I lean up and pull her breast into my mouth and bite down on the tip. She cries out as she comes, and I pull her down onto me three more times before I lose myself inside her.

She falls against my chest, and I close my eyes, feeling my heart beating wildly. "Did I hurt you?"

"No," she pants, giving my waist a squeeze, "but I doubt I'll be able to get out of this tub on my own."

I smile at her comment, then wait until I gather enough strength to get up while holding her. I set her on her feet just outside the tub, then grab a towel for her and wrap her up before hooking mine around my hips. I lead her to the bedroom, and once she's sitting on the edge of the bed, I reach into my nightstand and dig around until I find the box I'm looking for. I pull out the platinum ring with a large emerald-cut diamond and toss the box back in the drawer, then go to Chrissie, taking her left hand.

"Gus."

"If you're going to marry me, sweetheart, you're going to need this," I say, sliding the ring on her finger. The moment it's in place, I lift my head, and her eyes meet mine.

"How long have you had this?"

"Awhile. I was waiting for the right time to ask you. Seems now isn't just the right time—it's the perfect time."

"Oh my," she whispers, and then tears start to fall down her cheeks as she drops her eyes back to her hand. "Thank you."

"For what?"

"For pursuing me, for wanting me in spite of my quirks, and for loving me."

"Baby, you might not think you did, but you baited and landed me right in your trap by being everything you are."

"Well, then, it's a good thing I'm so awesome."

"Yeah, it is." I laugh, right before I kiss her, thinking I'm lucky as fuck I get to experience this kind of soul-deep happiness for the rest of my life.

Suggestion 18

SPREAD THE NEWS

CHRISSIE

I hold my hand to my stomach, praying that the nausea goes away, because it would really suck if I had to run for the restroom to avoid puking on Leah's kitchen table.

"I have news," Leah says, coming toward me with a glass of wine in one hand and a bottle of water in the other. The thought of wine makes my stomach roll, but I swallow the feeling and accept the glass, knowing I won't drink it. I still haven't told Leah I'm pregnant . . . actually, I haven't told anyone that Gaston and I are expecting. Part of me is still trying to come to terms with us becoming parents after only just accepting that I found the man of my dreams when I wasn't even looking.

"What news?" I ask.

"What is that?" she practically shouts, grabbing my wrist, and I barely have time to release the wineglass before she yanks my hand toward her. "Were you trying to keep this a secret?" At her question, my eyes fly to my finger as she flicks the beautiful ring sitting there from side to side.

"Of course not." I turn my hand over to grasp hers. "I just . . ." Do I say I forgot that I'm now engaged because I'm also pregnant and kinda focused on that because I'm seriously freaked out? "I'm trying to come to terms with things." I feel guilty for not sharing my engagement or my pregnancy . . . not that she and Tyler have been trying long.

She grins. "I understand coming to terms with things."

"You do?" I ask, and she laughs.

"Oh yeah." She wipes the hilarity from under her eye with the fingers from her free hand. "It wasn't exactly long ago that Tyler asked me to marry him." Her eyes take on a faraway look, and her voice is soft when she starts to speak again. "I remember being overwhelmed with fear and happiness at the same time." Her gaze, full of tenderness, locks with mine. "It all worked out, and now I cannot imagine things between us happening any differently. You'll feel the same; just give it some time."

"You're right. It's just . . ." I start to tell her I'm pregnant, but before I can get the words out, she steals them right from me.

"I'm pregnant."

I start to shake my head in disbelief. "You're . . . you and Tyler are pregnant?"

"Yes . . . and, well . . ." She grins. "We were wondering if you'd like to be godmother to him or her?"

"Oh my goodness."

"Is that a yes?"

"I . . ." I place my hand over my stomach and shake my head, whispering, "Oh my God."

I see the happy light in her eyes slide out as her features fill with confusion, and I know I need to pull myself together. "Do you . . . do you think you'd be up to returning that favor, along with taking on the job of my maid of honor?"

"What?" She looks confused.

"I somehow got myself knocked up, and I'm not only going to be a wife—I'm going to have a baby."

"Holy smokes," she whispers, and when she does my throat gets tight with tears. I try to hold them back, but I can't. I drop my gaze to my lap, and she lets my hand go before her chair slides back. When her arms wrap around me, I lift my arms and hold on to her tightly. "I'm guessing Gaston knows you're pregnant." I nod, unable to speak. "Is he happy?" I nod again, and her hand slides down my hair. "And . . ." I listen to her pull in a breath. "Are you happy?"

"I . . . I think so," I choke out, and she lets out the breath she's holding.

"You're scared."

"Yeah."

"A baby and an engagement is a lot to accept." She could say that again. "It's going to be okay. You're going to be okay."

"It's just . . . it's just that everything has happened so quickly."

Her arms tighten around me. "Everything has happened exactly how it's supposed to—it might not be normal or whatever, but you were supposed to meet Gaston, fall in love, and get pregnant. What you've found is rare and beautiful," she says, making me feel less freaked out about how everyone else might react when we tell them the news.

"You're right."

"You know I'm always here for you, right? You can talk to me about anything."

"I know." I give her waist a squeeze, then look up at her. "It's just I know you and Tyler have been trying, and this just kind of happened. I didn't want you to be upset, and I've been stressing out about how my mom is going to feel. She loves Gaston, but she might think it's too soon for us to have a baby."

She cuts me off with a shake of her head. "You're just like your dad."

"What?"

"He kept everything from you and your entire family, thinking he was doing the right thing." Oh God, he did do that, and I've done that more than once. "Like you told him, you have to let the people you love decide how they are going to react. You have to trust us to have your back, even if they might not like what is happening."

"It's seriously annoying that you're using my own words against me."

She smiles. "I love you. And I know why you didn't want to tell me you're pregnant, but you have to know, even if it never happened for me, I'd love you enough to still be happy for you."

"I'm a jerk."

"No, you just have a huge heart and want to protect everyone around you from anything that might hurt them. The thing is, we all want to do the same for you, so please let us."

"I'll try," I agree. Then I ask softly, "How happy is Tyler about the baby?"

Her face lights up, and her voice drops. "So happy."

"I'm happy for you two," I say, and she grins, then lets me go but only so she can grab my hand to once more examine my ring. My beautiful ring. A ring that the most amazing man in the world purchased with the idea of asking me to marry him before he even knew I was pregnant, because he wanted to spend the rest of his life with me.

"I'm happy for you too," she whispers, and her fingers tighten. "It's okay to be scared; it's also okay to be happy for yourself."

"I'm happy," I say, admitting to myself for the first time that the idea of carrying Gaston's baby makes me feel excitement instead of fear.

"You deserve happiness; you deserve everything good in life," she says, and my eyes slowly slide closed. "Enjoy it, girl."

"Oh my God," Mom whispers, staring at me unblinkingly. "Oh my God," she repeats, and Gaston's hand, wrapped tightly around mine, grows even tighter.

"Mom?"

"You're pregnant?"

"She just said she was," Chris says. He and Sam are on FaceTime. Sam shakes his head while bouncing my niece on his shoulder.

"We're happy for you, sis." Chris rolls his eyes at our mother, who hasn't said a word or blinked. Her reaction is making me seriously doubt Gaston's idea of sharing our news with my brother, Sam, and my mom at the same time.

"Mom, you're freaking me out."

"I'm going to be a grandma . . . again." She shoots out of her chair, tossing her arms in the air, and I laugh as she comes around the table to hug and kiss Gaston and me. "I'm so happy." She grabs my face and kisses my cheek. "So happy for both of you."

"So what do you say?" I ask, and my dad's eyes lift from his cup of coffee, where they dropped moments ago, and meet mine. The tears shimmering back at me make my heart ache in the best way.

"I'd be honored to walk you down the aisle," he says roughly. Tammy wraps her arm around his shoulders, then covers her mouth with her fingers and whimpers.

"Thank you, Daddy."

"Anything for you, honey." He reaches across the table to take my hand, and tears spring to my eyes as I reach out for him.

"Also, you guys should know you're going to be grandparents again," I say, and my dad's hand tightens around mine.

"Really?" Dad asks.

"Really," I say as Gaston's lips touch the side of my head.

"I'm so happy for you." He looks at Gaston. "Both of you."

"Really happy," Tammy says, and I smile at her.

"Mom, do you have a minute?" Gaston asks with his cell phone on speaker between us.

"Yeah, is everything okay?"

"Everything is great. Chrissie is here with me, and we have news."

"You're pregnant," she screeches, making me giggle. "I'll be there tomorrow."

"Mom."

"I need to go; I have to book my plane tickets. Love you, and see you both soon. Also, I'm so happy."

"We kind of got that," Gaston says drily, and I laugh as he hangs up the call.

I rest my hands against his chest and tip my head back. "Everyone knows."

"Everyone knows."

"Everyone is happy."

"Yeah." He touches his lips to mine; then I slide my arms around him and rest my head against his chest. My mom said she wanted me to find the kind of happiness that is soul deep, and I know I did just that.

Epilogue

HAPPILY EVER FOREVER

GASTON

With my daughter asleep in my arms and her mother asleep in the hospital bed, exhausted after sixteen hours of labor, I lower my lips to the top of my girl's head and breathe in her soft scent. After I've gotten my fill, I whisper quietly, "I wish you were here, Dad." I know he'd be happy for me. He'd be pleased that I found a woman like Chrissie to spend my life with, and he'd enjoy every second with his granddaughter.

"He's here." I lift my head and find my mom standing just feet away with a cup of coffee in her hand. I didn't even hear her come in.

"I know; I just wish Chrissie and Penelope had the chance to meet him."

"He's a part of you—one of the best parts of you—and for the rest of your life, you get to share him with your girls." She smiles sadly. "He was a good man."

"He was," I agree, and she nods as she comes closer.

"He'd be proud of you, not because you're as successful as you are but because you found someone worthy of you to share your life with. I'm glad he found that, too, before . . ." She cuts herself off as pain slices through her features. "I'm glad he found love." She reaches out for Penelope, and I carefully hand her over, watching as she curls my little girl against her chest. I study my mom—one of the most amazing and loving women I know—and hate that she's never allowed herself to share that love with anyone. When I was in my twenties, I asked her why she didn't want to settle down. She explained that after watching my grandmother stay in a marriage because it was the right thing to do and growing up in a home filled with resentment, she promised herself that she'd never settle.

"Will you ever be open to the idea of falling in love?" I ask her, and she lifts her eyes off my sleeping girl to smile at me.

"I fell in love the day you were born, and now, with Chrissie and this little one, I get to experience falling in love all over again." She kisses the top of Penelope's head, and I pull in a sharp breath. Hearing that, I realize something I haven't before. Both my mom and dad taught me about love and family in their own way. My mom taught me how to be happy on my own, and my father taught me to be open to the idea of love. I had the best of both worlds, and because of the two of them, I was able to recognize love when I found it.

"Love you," I say gruffly.

"I love you too," she whispers. I see every ounce of love she has for me shining so brightly that I feel it sear through me, and I hope when I look at my wife and my daughter they feel the exact warmth I'm feeling right now.

CHRISSIE

"Cheers." I hold my margarita glass out toward Leah, and she lifts hers out toward me, then stops.

"What are we toasting to?" she asks, and I look around her backyard at our growing families and say the first thing that comes to mind.

"Happiness."

"I'll definitely toast to that." She clinks her glass against mine, then takes a drink, and I do the same.

Hearing little girl giggles and angry boy shouts, I turn my head and sigh. Both Leah's daughter Corina and my sweet Penelope are chasing after Zach, Leah's almost-three-year-old son, and are trying to put a tiara on his head. The poor boy can't even make a proper escape, because the costume dress he has on keeps getting tangled around his feet, causing him to fall. I look from him to my boy Tobias, who's just a year old, and notice the girls have already dressed him up, and he's now sitting in the grass sucking on a red Popsicle and wearing a headband with little yellow antennas and a set of butterfly wings that actually look adorable on him. "Do you think we should stop the girls?" I ask, taking a sip of my drink.

"Probably," she says, not making a move to get up.

I smile at her, then laugh when I hear a rumbling "What the hell."

I turn to find Tyler and Gaston, who've been chatting, drinking beer, and manning the grill, spot their sons. The look on each of their faces is comical as they rush across the yard to rescue their boys from their daughters, who are convinced their brothers are living, breathing dolls. Leah and I didn't plan on having our kids at almost the same time, but nonetheless it happened, and I'm glad it did. Our girls are as close as sisters, and I know with time our boys will become the best of friends.

Tyler scoops up his son and places him on his hip, then bends to say something to his little girl and kisses the top of her head. Seeing that, my heart melts and my eyes start to water as Gaston gets down on the grass with our boy while our beautiful girl wraps her arms around his neck in a hug.

"I think we need another toast," Leah says quietly, and I pull my eyes off my entire world to look at her. "To the good life."

I hold up my glass. "To having it all."

"To having it all," she repeats, tapping her glass to mine.

I take a sip and watch my husband kiss our daughter until she laughs while our son giggles at the two of them. I really do have it all. I have a man who loves me completely, two beautiful children who make my life complete, and great friends and a huge family to share the good and bad with; on top of all that, I have a job I love. I couldn't ask for more.

Acknowledgments

First, I have to give thanks to God, because without him none of this would have been possible. Second, I want to thank my husband. I love you now and always—thank you for believing in me, even when I don't always believe in myself. To my beautiful son, you bring such joy into my life, and I'm so honored to be your mom.

To every blogger and reader, thank you for taking the time to read and share my books. There will never be enough ink in the world to acknowledge you all, but I will forever be grateful to each and every one of you.

Like thousands of authors before me, I started this writing journey after I fell in love with reading. I wanted to give people a place to escape where the stories were funny, sweet, and hot and left them feeling good. I have loved sharing my stories with you all, loved that I have helped people escape the real world, even for a moment.

I started writing for me and will continue writing for you.

XOXO,

Aurora

About the Author

Aurora Rose Reynolds is a *New York Times* and *USA Today* bestselling author whose wildly popular series include Until, Until Him, Until Her, and Underground Kings. Her writing career started as an attempt to get the outrageous alpha men in her head to leave her alone and has blossomed into an opportunity to share her stories with readers all over the world.

To stay up to date on what's happening, join the Alpha Mailing List: https://bit.ly/2GXYsVS. To order signed books, go to https://AuroraRoseReynolds.com. You can reach Reynolds via email at Auroraroser@gmail.com and follow her on Instagram (@Auroraroser), Facebook (AuthorAuroraRoseReynolds), and Twitter (@Auroraroser).